ISBN: 9798647233318
AUTHOR: EVA LEWIS
COPYRIGHT: 2020 by Eva Lewis. All Rights Reserved. Any questions can be directed to Eva Lewis at her website www.evllart.com

Prologue

A fire fumed nervously in the rain, and beings sat around it covered in black shadows. As they whispered to each other inside the dark alleyway, two clouds floated in from a corner. One of the shadowed figures looked over their shoulder at the clouds and nudged the others. They started to walk away reluctantly glancing back at their fire, this fire then morphed into a black Doberman dog, a red fire crackled from his paws and tail. A collar with a red ruby strung through it adorned his neck as he walked away from the small burning pit.

"Thanks..." He added, sitting down in front of the clouds.

"You're welcome, now where is Ara?" One of the clouds asked with authority morphing into a grey cat with an amethyst earring. There was fog swelling from his tail and paws.

"I can't say, everywhere?" The dog said, not at all phased by the new cat sitting in front of him. The other cloud transformed into another, lighter grey, cat with an aquamarine earring in her right ear.

"Clear up, Foggy!" She said, reaching a paw laced with mist and patting him on the head.

"Stop calling me that and start taking this seriously." The grey cat turned to face her, but before he did, a voice called from the sky.

"Sorry, I'm late, got flooded up in California." A grey-blue cat with blue markings walked around the corner, her fur soaking wet.

"It's fine. You're here now. Now tell me, have you found her?" The grey cat seemed reluctant to ask this.

"Yes, Fogstar," Her voice growing serious. "She is in a forest in Minnesota."

"AND?" The dog barked, jumping up to hover over the blue cat.

"SHH!" The white cat snapped as the dog sat back down.

"Good," Fogstar said impatiently, "I will leave to get her tomorrow, this world needs her help..."

An Odd Find

Rebecca sat in a chair, looking out the stained window of her cabin at the rain pattering down on leaves. She hated summer; it was supposed to be fun and happy. Playing with friends and skipping chores to get slushies at 7-11. But instead, she was in a cabin in the middle of nowhere with no freedom. Her family always went here in summer, a tradition she supposed. Her mother loved the open nature of Minnesota forests or whatever, and she missed her friends. Her hands held a torn journal that told a first-person story of how a girl and some guy saved a plane of existence or something. She didn't understand most of it because it was as if the author was writing it with no explanation or detail. One day just said, 'We crossed the river, and the Savoir lost her camera, she was despondent, but we have made it to Nostalgia. She likes it for some reason. A prophet told me I would spend a lot of time here; don't know what it means, but it's probably another little reason. We are staying at Present Hotel. No more to say, signed Fogstar, court recorder, and recipient of Queen Halo's advisory award.' Like what? The journal was ancient, and she was scared that it would just disintegrate in front of her. As this thought came to mind, her mother walked into the room from the kitchen door.

"Are you going to sit there and read that book all day?" She asked, the smell of smoky cooking latching onto her clothes.

"Well, what's wrong with that?" Rebecca teased, her mother smiled slightly.

"Nothing, but you need exercise, and it's a wonderful day today!"

"But Mom, its raini..." her mother cut her off.

"No buts, you're going outside."

Rebecca reluctantly went outside and quickly got drenched with rain. Her long brown hair was wet and dark, as was her striped pink and white shirt. Her Mom had rushed her out as fast as humanly possible, and she was now walking on the trail that linked up all the cabins in the forest. Rebecca wouldn't call it a forest, though. There were too many trees, and they closed in on you as you walked, giving off the impression that you were in a jungle. That was an excellent word for it, she thought, 'jungle.' A picnic table stood on her right, nothing special, but a glint of light reflected off of it. It was probably just the rain, but as she looked back, she saw something lying there. As she walked over to pick it up, she found it was a necklace, a diamond-cut rainbow necklace. She decided to keep it and walked the full loop before coming back to the cabin. The door creaked open, and inside she heard her brother talking to someone on the phone. The sound of sizzling food came from the kitchen.

"What do you mean, she switched classes?" Her brother, Jason, screamed at the poor soul who was on the other end. She pulled the necklace out of her pocket and examined it carefully. It was perfectly cut. Edges so sharp you could stab someone with them. Crystal points that looked organically man-made. The rainbow effect was outstanding, as well. No gem she had seen had something like this, and she supposed the person who lost it would be a least a little mad. She decided she'd keep it until tomorrow and try to find to whom it belonged. She put it around her neck and walked into her room through the steaming kitchen to her mother.

"Back so soon?" She asked, carrying a hot tray of cooked turkey and setting it down on the counter.

"Yeah, it started raining." She signaled herself, drenched with rain, and her mother nodded. As Rebecca started to her room Jason called out for her, she sighed and walked in.

"Hey, numbskull! How did you manage to…" Stopping after seeing the look on her face, which was pure confusion, he sighed angrily and hung up the phone. "You know Clara Seensfield?" He asked. Rebecca nodded. "Then, you know she changed classes?" Rebecca was confused but had no idea. Clara was a popular girl. She didn't know her personally, but before she could point this out, Jason seemed to notice. "Where did you get that?" He pointed at her necklace.

"I uh…" Rebecca started, but her mother calling for Jason, interrupted her, which was lucky. She went back to her room and prepared for dinner that night, as well as what to do tomorrow. She couldn't help feeling like Jason was lucky because of how much freedom he had. Plus, how many friends he could talk to over his beloved phone.

After dinner, she sat on her bed reading the same journal she found left in the house. The turkey had been okay, but Jason kept making off-handed complaints about Clara, which made everything worse. Rebecca had set the necklace on her nightstand and was looking out the window when her mom came in wearing a pink robe, with her brown hair tied up in a bun and a green face mask that looked half dry. She sat down next to Rebecca and smiled at her worriedly.

Questions

"So, Jason tells me you "found" something?"

Rebecca didn't know if she should deny it or not, but she didn't feel like acting out being surprised, she knew what "found" was supposed to mean. "No… I didn't *steal* anything." Her mother looked at her with her grey eyes, peering deep inside her soul.

"You're sure? I would be very disappointed in you if…" Rebecca cut her off.

"Just a cool leaf." She said, then snuggled into the covers of her bed. Her mother looked at her with suspicion. Rebecca pulled the journal from her bedside and opened it up to the page she was reading.

"What are you reading?" Her mother asked, scooting up next to Rebecca.

"I don't know, I found it in the cabin. It's weird, cause' it doesn't have any context, I think it's a diary." They read a few pages together, trying to find some explanation, but the closest thing they could see was the writer saying, 'The Queen has invited us for dinner tonight. We as her humble subjects have agreed graciously. The Savoir was quite happy when I bought her a new camera and…' it ended abruptly. The whole day ended with the pen trailing off, and there was nothing else besides one last paragraph. 'I feel a need to finish this off even if it… hurts. We won the war at the price of our Savior. That is all,' Her mother seemed disturbed by the contents of the book, she kissed Rebecca goodnight and headed out of the room.

Turning, she said, "Don't dwell on it too much; if you do, you might never fall asleep." A smile escaped both their mouths.

"I won't..." Rebecca said, curling up under her covers as the light clicked off above her. The darkness of her room carried her off to a dreamland of white triangles and foggy forests that curled away under pink light and sweet voices of comfort. Rain followed her everywhere, and black goop trailed behind as she tried desperately to catch up to the fading fog. She fell into holes that ended in the white lands of triangular mountains; the only thing getting her out was the sweet smell of time in her mouth that pushed her into black worlds of corrupted death. Misty, smoky, cloud-filled skies turned black and fell as the fog cried. Rebecca woke up with a start the next morning after her weird dreams. She seemed better rested than she had in a while and getting out of bed; she felt wonderful, even slipping into the same clothes from yesterday felt like a good thing.

She walked out of her room, met with a tasty breakfast and a bright new day.

Meeting Fogstar

Rebecca was walking around the loop, trying to find the owner of the necklace. She had walked around twice to see if anyone was out looking for it, but the only people she saw were runners or people walking their dogs. It was still raining, just a drizzle now, but she was half soaked. The leaves from fallen trees framed the gravel path she was walking on; some landed in her hair but quickly fell off as she was walking. A rustle in the bushes beside her stopped her for a second, but she kept walking anyway. It was nothing special. There were animals in the forest; she supposed it was just a rabbit or something. A minute later, she heard it from another bush beside her; she walked for another minute, and another, and another, until she couldn't stand it any longer and had to look. She walked over to the side of the path with the strange feeling of doing something right for the world and pulled back the wet leaves to reveal nothing but fog? There was just a single patch of it in the middle of nowhere with no explanation. Rebecca pushed leaves aside to look behind the bush for a smoke machine or something, but none were there. She pushed the leaves back again, expecting the same thing, but instead, there was a cat, a weird looking cat with grey fur, and an amethyst earring in its left ear. It slowly walked out of the bush with a calmer expression than Rebecca thought it should have and sat down in front of her. Then, out of all the things it could've done, it *talked*.

"Miss Rebecca, I presume?" The cat said, staring up at her. Before Rebecca could scream at this sudden action, he spoke again. "Are you?" He asked. She stared at him for what seemed like forever, his grey eyes laced with the pains of hundreds of years. They were a lighter grey than his fur, which looked combed and cut to a desirable length. The shape of the earring was like a diamond; it glinted and reflected the sun above.

"Wha…" She stammered at him, he tilted his head and looked at her with suspicion.

"I would be in a lot of trouble if you were not… oh dear, have I gotten the wrong one?" A slight panic edged the ends of his voice as it fell over her like morning fog.

"No, I- what?" She tried to ask, but he rolled his eyes and sighed.

"I am Fogstar, a being of utmost authority. I am here to take you to queen Halo. You wouldn't refuse such a gracious offer from the Queen now would you? Please, if you will allow me." He lit up like a light that grew brighter and brighter until Rebecca couldn't see anymore. The sound of wind rushed and filled her ears, and she left this realm.

Emphasis

Rebecca felt a furry paw on her face. She was on her back, staring up at the sky, it was bright blue, and the clouds were a lovely shade of fluffy white. Trees surrounded her, tall, dark trees of every color imaginable, pink, white, and blue. Their leaves spread across the ground framing the grass she sat on, which was...

"Finally," A voice cut off her thoughts. "I do not know why Ara thought that Emphasis was a good place to bring you. It is not very easy to stray your mind away from the..." Rebecca sat up, her head hurt, and her vision was foggy. The cat was staring at her with an expression of annoyed worry. Rebecca almost screamed as she came to her senses. There was a talking cat and a much more colorful city than community guidelines would ever allow. Had she just been kidnapped? "Try not to think of this place too much; Emphasis makes quite the impression on newcomers... Ara..." He sighed and looked up at her.

"Wha-" He cut her off.

"Where are you?" He asked for her. She nodded slowly, scanning the houses and fountains and the bridge that led into, what looked like, a town square.

"Let me explain..." She looked back towards him, and he sat down. "As I said, I am Fogstar. You are now in the Astral Plane and will be defeating Nightshade for the good of all realms. We are currently in Emphasis and will be meeting a group of beings. Halo, the queen, assigned me to get you here." He said, looking at her expectantly. She just looked at him, her mouth open slightly. The way he said those words was rehearsed, like he'd done them, begrudgingly, before. He didn't sound like he wanted to be doing this now either, his patience seemed to slip as she stared at him. "You do not understand, do you?" He sighed and went on. "Look, I am hoping to make this quick, so please pay attention, ask questions if you need to. Just listen, you are in the Astral Plane, you were in the Physical Realm, or Earth as you mortals call it. Here, where you are right now, we have a problem. Nightshade, a corrupt evil being, has decided he wants to take everything over. You, as the Savior, will be stopping him. Do you understand?"

"What the... how are you talking? What are...? Where..?" She stammered. He stared at her for a second then summoned a cloud of fog that pushed her to her feet.

"I do not have time for this; just come with me." He said, leading her down to a bridge made of oak. Giant pink flowers and green vines intertwined with the railing keeping beings from falling into the rushing crystal clear water below. As they walked across, a colossal fountain made of creamy white cement with flowing pink water that cascaded downward, tiny little details came into focus, houses of all shapes and sizes with rainbows of flamboyant color spreading across them. The cat led through the town filled with animals and people with weird defects and clothes that didn't make any sense at all. At one point, she saw someone with insect wings fly off the ground to hang up decorations. The further they walked, the more confusing things got. The animals got weirder, the people grew more disturbing, and the housing got more and more unrealistic. Giant pads of crystal lined sidewalks, as misshapen figures walked out of their bright beams to the happy faces of friends. Shops lined streets of marbled rock while colorful lights shined overhead, causing rays of color to shoot to the ground. In truth, it was beautiful here; it was like someone had taken a highlighter and scratched it all over the town. Rebecca didn't trust the place, it was too happy. The cat led her down more walkways before stopping at an alleyway and looking towards Rebecca with another expression of bored worry.

"Are you sure you are okay? You seemed distressed."

"OF COURSE I'M DISTRESSED I DON'T KNOW WHERE I AM OR WHO YOU ARE OR HOW YOU'RE TALKING OR WHY-" He floated up to her using another cloud of fog and put a paw on her mouth, silencing her as passing beings gave her odd looks.

"Those questions, most of them, I have already answered. I can and will do so again, but we need to get to a more secure place to talk. Inside are a few of my friends who the queen has requested to become stopping points on our journey. They have helped put together most of what is going on right now, and they are currently expecting us." He signaled the alleyway, which was dark and had the faint smell of burning rain and mist. He had a serene expression, which calmed her down slightly; she turned to look around again as the cat looked at her. "You do not trust me, do you?" He asked.

"No, you're a cat that can talk."

"And?" He said, taken aback. "Well, I suppose they do not do that where you are from, do they?" He sighed and floated back down to the ground. "Come inside; they are waiting. I am sure Mistral has probably already torn up the place in anticipation." He walked inside the alley covering him in darkness; Rebecca hesitated before stepping in as well, the dark threw her into a slight panic before she reached a lighter patch where the cat was sitting. He was looking at her with a fond expression that turned quickly to guilt as he knocked on the end of the brick alley's wall.

Meeting the Group

The smell of wet fur and fire was stronger here. It was a… different smell. Rebecca still didn't understand what was going on here, but she figured the cat knew what he was doing.

"Who's there?" A voice, clearly female, asked from behind the wall.

"Fogstar," The cat said, Rebecca's heart was pounding. "And our new Savior." Lights turned on from above, and the wall slid back to reveal a stone room. It looked like a cave, books, scrolls, and gems lined the walls filled with bookcases and cushions. A few beings were standing or sitting around the room. There was an grey-blue cat with navy markings on her face. She was soaked with water, a

Doberman dog with blazing fire coming out of the tips of his ears and tail, as well as his paws, finally a cat that looked like Fogstar but with longer unkempt fur and an aquamarine earring in her right ear.

"Oh, wow…" The blue cat said, walking up to her and circling her. "She's perfect. Did you find her where I told you to?" Fogstar nodded his head and stared up at Rebecca impatiently.

"These are Halo's assigned beings that will be helping us. Ara," He said, pointing at the blue cat. "She handles the rain. Blaze," He indicated the dog. "Handles the smaller forest fires and things like that. Mistral," He pointed at the grey cat. "My sister, she handles the mist. And as you know, I am Fogstar, and as you should have guessed, I handle the fog."

"Wait," Rebecca said, confused. "So everything that happens on Earth is caused by - you?"

"What E-Ear tth?" Ara tried.

"No, Earth, it's what the mortals call the Physical Realm." Fogstar said, Ara gave an 'ohhhh' and continued examining Rebecca. "And yes, we are the Personification of things that happen on… Earth…"

"So, you could end all the fires, and floods, and…" She paused, wondering if this was true or not, "Death?"

"Yes," Fogstar said simply. "But if we stop for too long or do it too often we will…" He trailed off. "Well I'll say fired is accurate." He added before crawling into a corner and pulling out a scroll.

Best Laid Plans

"Soooooooo..." Mistral said in an impatient voice.

"So, we will be planning our route, taking that route, and getting to Halo's Tower." Fogstar calmly answered as he scribbled on the piece of parchment placed in front of him.

"But that's so boring!" Mistral said. The others had explained she was Fogstar's older sister. They had described a lot in the time it took for Fogstar to -- well, map out their route? They had said that the Astral Plane was a different plane of existence, obviously, from the Physical Realm where Rebecca lived and the Astral Plane where everyone else did. In this Astral Plane Nightshade, the old ruler, corrupted by a stone of pure evil, that's what they said anyway, wanted to take over everything, and someone needed to stop him. They said that person was her.

"Hey... Fogstar?" She asked. He lifted his head to look at her. "Do you have any other siblings?"

"OH!" Mistral said excitedly, "Your BRILLIANT! You guys can stop by Smokescreen and maybe..." she paused, looking over at Fogstar. "You two can get along for once in your lives?"

"NO! No, no, absolutely not! I will never go to that foul little liar's house ever again; he almost got us killed last time!" He snapped at her.

"Oh dear, what happened between him and his brother?" Ara asked Blaze, who shrugged awkwardly. "I've been gone a long time... Hurricanes and..."

"Oh no, they've hated each other for like… well longer than your absence, that is. It's just gotten…" Mistral looked over at the brooding cat as Blaze said, "Worse." Mistral smiled awkwardly as Ara nodded her head and started talking to Blaze.

"So, you have more siblings?" Rebecca asked, causing Fogstar to throw a look of hatred at Mistral before walking off to get something off a bookshelf.

"Yeah," Blaze said slowly, looking over his shoulder to make sure Fogstar wasn't listening, "Smokescreen is the oldest, Mistral is the middle child, then Fogstar." Blaze said simply. "Smokescreen is… an irresponsible being." Fogstar returned and spread a few of what looked like maps across the table.

"Alright, Miss, we shall be covering the route now. Does this look fine?" She looked down at the map and was stunned at the detail. "To get this cleared up, you shall be traveling with me…" As Rebecca looked at the tiny towns and cities dotted across the paper, she realized that this was miles of land to cross.

"Wait, this is like a whole continent. Do you have a car?" Rebecca asked. Most of the beings in the room seemed not to know what a car was. Even Fogstar seemed the slightest bit confused.

"What's a car?" Ara asked, but Fogstar waved her off and answered for her.

"No, I do not have a *car*. We shall be walking though I assure you it will not be long, a week or two, maybe, if we're lucky, we will get a head-start." Rebecca followed the dotted red line through the Astral Plane to what would be the end of their journey, a large grey tower with a yellow crystal and town around it.

"A week or two?" She was distracted by how the map seemed to be expanding and changing.

"Is that too long?" Blaze asked, crossing the room to look at the map. "Hey, you're stopping by my house?"

"They're gonna go to everyone's place," Mistral said, picking something out of her teeth with one sharp claw.

"One question, why does he have to do it? Can't I go alone or like -- what am I even supposed to be doing anyway?" Fogstar seemed offended by Rebecca's first question.

"I am your *escort*..." He said. Mistral in the background snorted before looking away and pretending to be interested in the ceiling. "It would be very confusing if you went alone, let alone dangerous." He paused, seeming to find a flaw in his work and going back to adjust the map.

"As to what you're doing here Dear, Defeating Nightshade, of course!" Ara said, sipping on a cup of tea that appeared out of thin air.

"Right... what? How? I still don't understand completely..."

"Then may we give you some context?" Fogstar asked, setting his pencil down. "Ara, we will need your visions..." Ara smiled and got up; she sat down next to Fogstar. The markings on her face started to glow as she handed Rebecca a cup of hot tea that swirled around the sides carefully.

Stories

"Alright…" Ara said, she closed her eyes and held her breath. As the blue markings on her face glowed still brighter, Fogstar began to talk.

"About a hundred years ago, a being named Nightshade turned evil. He was the king of the Astral Plane, ruling alongside our queen Halo." The alleyway they stood in suddenly turned into a haze that transformed into a black shadow of a cat sitting on a throne next to a beaming white one. A sea of concrete and cheering beings surrounded them; it then turned dark. "He found some kind of crystal on an expedition, destroyed since then, but the effects remain present on our past king." The vision showed the black cat reaching out to a stone as his eyes turned orange, and the cave around him turned into black goop. "He soon tried to take over the Astral Plane, as such overthrowing Halo as queen. We had to raise an army and" Rebecca cut him off.

"You talk about it like you were around back then." The vision faded away as Rebecca sipped on her tea.

"We were; we all were," Blaze said, tilting his head to look at her as she spat out her tea onto the rug.

"How old *are* you?" She asked, Ara had a worried look on her face, but Fogstar was the one to respond.

"It depends; we are all created for a purpose. The guardians are different from us, but -- you do not understand any of this do you, Miss?" Rebecca shook her head. "Let us finish, and then we can answer those questions, alright?" The world faded into an army of beings following the white cat. "We uh… won that war, but Nightshade was not defeated forever and -- well, that is why you are here. You are going to defeat him this time." The vision blurred, and the white cat turned into the silhouette of a girl in white. As the world faded back into a stone alley and Ara opened her eyes smiling, she realized they were serious. She stared at all the faces looking at her.

"It might be a lot to take in…" Ara said sympathetically, as the cup in her hand filled itself with swirling tea.

"Uhhh…" Rebecca said, staring at them all.

"Alright other questions you might have?" Fogstar said, stepping over to his map and tweaking a few more lines. Rebecca sat there, staring at her cup for a few seconds before Fogstar looked up at her and sighed.

"First off, there are two kinds of beings in the Astral Plane. One is us. We are personifications of certain things in the Physical Realm -- Earth. We make things happen, such as me making the fog. If I do not do my job, there is no fog, anywhere. Then there are the guardians, they protect one human for that human's life, and when it dies, they can either choose to retire or to get another human. We call them Mortals here, please be reminded of that so that you do not seem too suspicious." He stopped and looked up at her again. "Are you alright, Miss?"

"I have to kill someone?" The whole room went quiet as she stared at her cup in shock. Why her? How would she do it? Should she do it? She had too many questions overwhelming her.

"Well…" Mistral said, worriedly walking over to Fogstar, who had his eyebrows furrowed and was staring at his paws.

"Yes." He said. There was anger in his voice that seemed to scare everyone. "That's the plan, get rid of him. If that means killing him, then that is what we have to do." He paused. "Though I doubt it will come to that…" He got up and walked over to Rebecca. "Do you have any more questions?"

"Why me?" Rebecca asked.

"Who knows?" Mistral said, returning to her regular hyper self, floating on her back in mid-air. Fogstar cleared his throat, and she snickered, sitting back down on a ledge.

"We do not know why but you are who Halo said to give that to." Fogstar pointed at the necklace she was wearing. "Do not ask what it does; you will find out later. For now, we do need to go find some goods to bring with us." The wall disintegrated as Fogstar walked up to it, he beckoned her onwards. Rebecca looked around at the other beings; they seemed completely fine with the idea of letting a 15-year-old kill an evil magic cat. Fogstar poked his head around the corner and waved her forward.

"I'm only fifteen, and you're letting me do this?" Ara spat out her tea. Blaze's mouth dropped open, and Mistral looked at her like she didn't hear her correctly. Fogstar grabbed her arm and dragged her out as everyone looked around, thinking they misheard her.

More Emphasis

"Fifteen is quite young here, Miss... if you could avoid saying your age, for now, that would be better." Fogstar said as he led her around town again. They entered some kind of shopping center full of beings. Every window was full of products, gifts, cameras, sweets, and all sorts of other things, Rebecca had no idea what they were. Fogstar led her across one of the golden streets into a lavender-colored building with a massive door. It seemed to be selling astral sweets because none of them looked like food, but the faces of the other beings made her think otherwise as they ate their candy. Fogstar walked up to the counter and made himself float to reach eye level with the woman at the front. She had bubblegum colored hair and a powdery apron. Rebecca could've sworn she saw a fluffy pink tail swish behind her.

"Good morning, may we..." Fogstar looked up at the menu and then looked at Rebecca. "Do you know what chocolate is?" The girl nodded sweetly and reached under the counter.

"It's strange how many beings have asked for that since the last..." She said, but Fogstar cut her off by clearing his throat. The smile disappeared off her face as she stuffed bars of chocolate glazed with a white sauce into a little bag. She folded it and handed it to him. "That will be seven gold coins." Fogstar summoned a cloud of fog and pulled out seven-round gold coins; he gave them to her, said thank you, and dragged Rebecca out of the shop.

"Here." Fogstar broke a piece in half and gave one to her; he stuffed the other part back in the bag and into a new cloud of fog. It tasted surprisingly good for a copy of a

Hershey's bar. Fogstar led her into different stores around town, buying things and pulling coins out of clouds. Rebecca was surprised at how much money he was spending on her. When she tried to ask him why they needed so many things he told her they were "necessities", but when he led her into what looked like a gift shop called Yelts and told her to get anything, she doubted that was the case. She didn't get anything there, but when Fogstar insisted, she decided that a lovely baby pink Polaroid camera would do well. But she set it back down when she saw the look of despair in Fogstar's face. After packing everything into a cloud and saying goodbye to Ara, Mistral, and Blaze, Fogstar told her it was time to go. He led her to an archway of gold bricks, and he walked to the other side, pausing for a little red beam to shoot out and then flash green before retreating to the other side. Rebecca did the same, and Fogstar started walking with her following in his paw-prints.

Leaving

They had been walking for at least an hour when Fogstar told her that they had just left Emphasis even though it had been, well, at least an hour. Rebecca gave him a skeptical look before he smiled to himself and began to talk.

"Each town had room to expand without touching the other cities, as the Astral Plane expands continually." The towering pines and spruces around them shivered as Fogstar added. "The forests and other areas that are uninhabited stay the same as well." Mist crawled between the trees and spread onto the gravel path they were walking along.

"Oh... well, where are we now?" Rebecca looked down at Fogstar, who was smiling at the mist.

"Serenity Forest." He said, looking up at the sky before looking back at her. "Most places in the Astral Plane invoke a certain emotion or feeling inside of beings." The trees along the path seemed to back away and let them walk as they spent their time talking about where to go and how things happened, or where the Astral Plane was and why no one knew it existed. Fogstar had apologized and shrugged, telling her he had no idea besides the fact that they had magic and mortals didn't, which explained a lot in her opinion. When the sky turned cloudy, and rain started to fall as afternoon time came upon them, the feeling of tranquility amplified ten-fold. Fogstar was silent for a long time before Rebecca finally asked where they were going, he looked ahead at the trail that faded into a grey smear.

"We are heading to the next town over, Ease, and then to the Wetlands. That's where Ara lives." He added, glancing at the holes between trees sniffing the air warily.

"So Ease is... as big as Emphasis? And the Wetlands are...?" She asked, glancing at the trees and then back at Fogstar.

"Ease is almost as big as Emphasis; the Wetlands are more of an area to build your house on. It's less of a town and more of an area like Serenity Forest, but instead, more people choose to live there." Fogstar said, taking one last look at the tree before returning his gaze to the path. As they walked, someone was watching them. Rebecca had no idea Fogstar knew.

A Trail to Follow

They followed the trail for a long time before anything interesting happened. Fogstar had seemed wary the whole time, but Rebecca thought nothing of it. She assumed he was just paranoid. The pine trees wafted their sweet scent towards Rebecca as the sky swirled above them, causing the serene effect to be even more apparent. It was a nice walk; she looked down at Fogstar, who was looking at the ground with a focused expression. His ears were straight up and seemed to be listening for something. As Rebecca finished her judgment about Fogstar being paranoid, a black figure jumped out of the bushes and tackled Fogstar. A few drops of black goop spattered the ground and Rebecca as the thing, which seemed to be a black animal dripping in goo, got thrown out of the fight and then ran back in. It and Fogstar got tangled in a ball of hissing and claws that Rebecca couldn't make out, she tried to help, but every time she did, she got thrown back by one of Fogstar's clouds. A light bloomed from the clouds and a scroll hit the ground with a soft thud. Finally, a loud yowl filled the air, and the black thing got thrown out of the circle with an expression of the utmost hatred. It slinked away into a bush growling softly at Fogstar, covered in bloody scratch marks. He eyed the bush for a few seconds before sitting down and licking the blood off one of his paws.

"WHAT WAS THAT?" Rebecca screamed, backing away from the trees; Fogstar flinched at the loud noise.

"One of Nightshade's followers." He said, merely looking over to the trees again and sniffing the air to make sure it had left.

"AND- WH- UGHHH-" Rebecca threw her hands up to cover her face before looking down at Fogstar. "I have to fight those things?"

"Yes?" Fogstar said, looking at her with confused eyes and licking more blood from his shoulder.

"Are you okay?" She asked, expecting a verbal answer. Instead he shrugged, flinched and went back to tending his wounds. She was going to comment on how apathetic that was, but Fogstar got up and walked over to the scroll sitting on the ground.

"Now, let's see about this...

Scroll

Fogstar opened the scroll very carefully as if it would break at any moment. He scanned the first few lines before handing it to Rebecca. She took it gingerly and held it to her face as the rain stopped landing on her.

Hello Dear Savior

Please excuse my interruption of the trip but I just had to write to you

I'm so sorry for the way they broke the news to you

Fogstar can be a bit harsh to other beings

Now if you can I would like to know some things about you

What's your name? How do you like the Astral Plane? As for your guide, how do you like him?

Please write back when you can, please and thank-you

Signed, Sealed, Loved, and Fathomed

Halo

"When are we going to get to that town?" Rebecca asked, rolling the scroll back and tying the little gold string around it.

"Why do you ask?" He got up and winced, shaking a few drops of blood everywhere. "Tonight."

"Are you sure you can walk all the way?" Fogstar scowled at her, stood up, and walked three feet away. She gave him a worried look and walked down the road with him. He kept sniffing the air; she guessed it was to see if there were any more of Nightshades' followers. As the day bled into night and stars started zooming across the sky, Fogstar spoke again.

"We should be there soon, just an hour or two more…" He sniffled what looked like a bloody nose in the dark and kept walking without complaint. Rebecca figured that Fogstar had experienced worse injuries than this but was still surprised at his vigilance. The trees darker than usual backed away from the trail warily as they kept walking.

Ease

They had walked for what seemed like an hour and a half, and just as Fogstar said, they approached a giant wall that looked to be three or four stories tall. It was made out of wooden logs and seemed not to have a single entrance around the whole thing.

"How do we get through?" Rebecca stared up at the top of the wall, which had little lanterns.

"Just walk through, it isn't real," Fogstar said as he fazed through the wall like it was a hologram. Rebecca hesitated before shoving her hand through. When it didn't hit the wall or get cut off, she stepped through and felt a wave of comfort surge through her. She gazed at beings dressed in sweatpants and tee-shirts, all looking relaxed and care-free, except for the fact that all of them were staring at Fogstar with expressions of the utmost horror. Fogstar was standing by the wall with one eyebrow raised, staring back in confusion.

"What?" He asked, looking around at everyone staring at him. Some even had their hands over their mouths or worried tears filling their eyes.

"Oh my..." A lady with coral colored hair tied up into a ponytail said while staring at them in horror. A basket full of fruits and papers draped in rose-colored silk around her arm had been dropped to the ground in shock. Rebecca noticed the comfortable looking nurse's outfit and realized why they were all staring.

"I don't think they're used to seeing hurt beings..." Rebecca whispered to Fogstar, she saw his eyes widen, and his ears go straight down. The nurse walked up to them with a fearful expression.

"Oh dear, we must get you to the hospital. How are you walking? Oh no, no, no..." She grabbed their hands as Fogstar tried to convince her not to take them.

"No, really, I'm fine. It's just a sraaAAAaAHHhHHhH!!!" She pulled them off towards the nearest hospital with Fogstar screaming and pleading not to go, that he was fine. Rebecca was going too fast to see the rest of the town, but from what she saw, it was charming with little fairy lights hanging from lamp posts that hung small lanterns. Square houses lined the streets with soft yellow lights pouring onto the grainy streets. It was a beautiful town. Fogstar was also right about the size, almost as big as Emphasis. The hospital wasn't large considering that nobody in this town ever got hurt, but it was obvious that the three or four nurses tending to Fogstar all night were very good at their job. At least that's what it looked like sitting next to the bed they put Fogstar in. He kept telling them that he was fine as they shoved medicine into his mouth, telling him to calm down, or he might hurt himself. At a point, he must've given up because he resorted to refusing the pills and pouting. Rebecca sat, gazing out the window on the far side of the room with a lingering question on her mind. As the hours of insisting and clambering sounds droned on, Rebecca felt her-self slipping away. She fell asleep, staring out the window.

The next morning she felt terrifically tired. A haze of pale yellow light filtered into the windows as passing beings went out for their shopping or meetings with other beings. Fogstar had fallen asleep at some point, and the nurses said not to bother him, so instead, she walked around the small halls trying to find where breakfast was as her stomach curled with hunger. After walking around for a while, she decided that it was a lost cause and stumbled around until she found Fogstar's room. Another nurse was trying to force feed him a spoon filled with thick green liquid.

"I am fine. See look, no more cuts or anything, totally fine." He said, the nurse gave up and walked out the room smiling helplessly at Rebecca.

"Hey, what's for breakfast?" Rebecca asked. The nurse turned her head to look at her before scuttling away to find something to eat.

"Ease has the most worrisome beings in the whole Astral Plane," Fogstar sneered, taking off the heap of bandages on his body. The nurse clicked her white heels into the room carrying a tray of Astral foods Rebecca had never seen before. She picked up a piece of golden fruit and took a bite. It was pretty good, it tasted like a peach. She held out a slice of cake to Fogstar, who shook his head and walked over to the window seal.

"As I mentioned before this is Ease. I'm sorry we didn't get a real hotel." He gave an annoyed look at the door. He must've seen the blank expression on Rebecca's face because he asked. "What is wrong, Miss?"

"Fogstar... When am I going to go home?" She saw his ears go back and his eyebrows rose.

"Well, I-" He started to respond but stopped in the middle with a look of pessimistic doom; he looked around the room before taking a deep breath and answered her question again. "I am not going to lie to you; I do not know if you will be able to. Of course, if you defeat Nightshade, you will have to leave, but..." He trailed off, looking out the window. "You will save us all, and then you can go home." Maybe she wanted to go home now and not fight him. She wondered if she could do that, for a few seconds, not realizing how stupid it was. She glanced at Fogstar; he stared out the window, clearly worried for her wellbeing.

Behind

They got out of the hospital about an hour later; it had taken a lot of insisting from Fogstar, but they had done it. After walking around town under the cozy sun and fairy lights, they reached a drizzling fountain and sat down on a backless bench in front of it. Fogstar looked around at the beings sniffing the air while Rebecca stared lazily at the fountain. She was quite tired, having slept so long; she figured it was Ease's fault that she overslept. She forced her eyes back open and stared out into the distance.

"We need to leave; Nightshade's followers know we are here. I do not think it would be a good idea to get stuck in a town with them." Fogstar said, gazing around before turning his head to see Rebecca nod her head lazily. His expression flattened as he patted her arm, she jumped up, fully awake now. They got up and walked for a few extra minutes, passing cafés and stores, houses and stands full of blankets and comfort food. As the street cleared and they moved back out the other end of the big wooden wall, they came across a toll bridge on the other side. A small red booth, supposedly to lower the bridge, sat next to a road of cement crossing over a gurgling river of silvery water. A sleeping guard with bright orange hair and freckles was sitting in an office chair inside the booth. Fogstar cleared his throat as the man sat bolt upright and smiled sleepily at them.

"What services do you require, kind sir?" He said in a voice that sounded like smooth silk, it lulled Rebecca, and she almost fell over in a trance.

"Would you lower the bridge for us?" Fogstar said, sounding utterly unfazed by the comforting hug of the town's sleepiness accompanied by the sounds of the river rushing by the rustling trees as the birds chirped. Fogstar had to elbow Rebecca again to keep her awake.

"Course, that'll be two gold coins." The man smiled at them and wrote something down on a piece of paper while Fogstar summoned a fog cloud and pulled out two golden-colored coins. Fogstar slammed them onto the counter, causing the man and Rebecca to snap out of their trance. The man grabbed the coins and put them in a cash register before pulling a lever and lowering the bridge. "The names Toll, by the way." He tipped his red uniform hat and let them go. Rebecca's feet were sticking to the mushy ground as the feeling of comfort swept from her like the river flowing behind them and faded into the distance replaced by the sound of squishing grass and squawking crows.

The Wetlands

Droopy trees dotted the landscape of the swampy wilderness they had been walking in. There was no path, but Fogstar seemed to know just where to go anyways. Cattails lined the small ponds of murky water they passed every so often with the sun beating down heat that made Rebecca fan herself, self-consciously. She felt wet; it might have been just sweat.

"I'm guessing this is the Wetlands." Rebecca looked around at the temperate landscape cautiously; she noticed the ground was getting wetter.

"Yes, we will be stopping by Ara's house." Fogstar said, looking up at her with the expression of a tour guide. "The Nightshade followers will not attack us here; the one in Serenity Forest was just a scout, besides they know Ara lives here. So we should be relatively safe, Miss."

"You can call me Rebecca." She looked down at him as his ears pressed back.

"Yes, sorry." He said. The area around them was changing now too; more trees blocked the sun out of Rebecca's face causing the heat level to plummet. They saw water pools more often, and they had to walk around at least three, the cattails prickling Rebecca's ankles as she passed. "Ara lives here?" Fogstar perked up at this question.

"Yes, she and her mother have lived here for as long as I can remember, and that is a long time mind you." He said, taking an extra-long stride to keep up with Rebecca's faster pace, it was much cooler now, she felt like she was in a pool, a crystal clear, fresh pool.

"Ara has a mom?" Fogstar nodded in response. "Who are your parents?" Fogstar stopped in his tracks with an expression of guilt.

"I uh... do not have any. Or at least no one knows who they are..." Rebecca apologized to him profusely after this. He said it was okay and directed them to an abandoned campsite not far from the road they were traveling on. It had a beige tent and a campfire that Fogstar lit hesitantly. He looked half asleep by the time he entered the tent a few minutes later, but kept up conversation perfectly well and didn't seem to have any problems even when the daylight bled out of the sky. He still insisted on keeping guard until morning. Rebecca fell asleep with the sounds of rustling leaves and misty dew filling her lungs. She slept soundly that night, only disrupted by the sounds of screeching owls or the occasional growl outside from Fogstar.

Ara's House

When she woke up, warm-colored light was pouring in through the door, and Fogstar was outside looking up at the sky with an expression of bliss. He didn't even turn around; he just got up and started walking away as the fire was already out, he was considerate enough to leave the tent up. They spent an hour or two walking through the marsh before Rebecca finally said something.

"So how long have we been, uh... traveling?" Fogstar glanced up at her and then held a paw up to count.

"In all two days and five hours." He said, quickly changing his course a few paces to the left.

"Already?" Rebecca said, scooting back next to him as he nodded his head and took a sharp right, stopping in front of a house. Its dark wooden walls covered in moss and vines with hanging white flowers. Two waterfalls spilled on either side, pouring into small ponds of silky dark water filled with lily pads and cattails. Stairs led up to the door of the house, which was suspended above wet grass by thin stilts. Fogstar stepped up to the door and knocked on it three times. They heard the sound of damp paw prints rushing up to invite them in.

"Oh, you're right on time!" Ara said, smiling and looking to a golden clock on the wall. It was much bigger on the inside, blue curtains swung by open windows, and water dripped from the ceiling, making the blue-grey carpet soaking wet.

"Always. Do not doubt my time management." Fogstar said. Ara laughed as she poured tea into three cups interlaced with patterns of cherry blossoms.

"How was the travel?" Ara asked, handing a cup to Fogstar, who sat down on a couch in front of a golden table.

"We got attacked on the way to Ease, was to be expected, though. I swear, the nurses there..." Fogstar grumbled, Rebecca sat down next to him. Ara sat down on a magenta pillow in front of them; she smiled at them, taking a sip from her cup.

"So Blaze's battle predictions were correct?" She asked. Fogstar nodded lazily, taking a sip of his tea and starting to set it down. He hesitated and made a coaster of fog before placing it on the table. Ara held out a cup to Rebecca, she took it and said thank-you to Ara who smiled at her and nodded. Rebecca took a sip and realized that the house was gone. When she looked up, it was a café full of heavy-looking greenery and white flowers. It smelled like coffee grounds and the ocean, as it faded away she looked at Ara.

"What's in the tea?" She asked, unsurely setting it down on the table. Fogstar threw a glance at it before shoving another coaster under it.

"Oh, it's Vision Tea... do you not like it?" Ara asked, leaning forward to take the cup from her, but Rebecca stopped her.

"No, I love it, it's just that we don't have stuff like that in the..." She looked over at Fogstar, who was calmly enjoying his tea now. "Physical Realm."

"The Physical Realm has food, but it is not vision," Fogstar said, looking out the window softly sniffing the air again.

"How do you live without vision foods?" Ara looked as if she would've liked to say sorry for living somewhere like Earth.

"Well, I never knew they..." She realized Ara didn't know very much about how the world worked, did she? "You don't know much about Earth, do you?"

"Physical Realm." Fogstar corrected her, taking another sip. Ara shook her head sadly.

"No, not really. I don't go down there often; I like to hang out with Cloudjumper while raining, but I go down to the surface sometimes."

"Would you like me to tell you about it?" Rebecca asked. Fogstar glanced at her with a pitiful expression. Ara looked up and smiled widely.

"Yes, please, I've always wanted to know why mortals do all those things," Ara said excitedly, she set her cup down on the table as Fogstar shoved another fog coaster under it.

"Well, what would you like to know?" Rebecca glanced down at Fogstar, who choked on his tea.

"Oh well... lots of things, actually..." Ara trailed off, staring at the ceiling with a face of bliss. Rebecca knew what was coming; she looked down at Fogstar, who was looking up at her pitifully. She sighed as Ara adjusted herself in her seat and cleared her throat.

Earthly Questions

Ara sat thinking for a few seconds and then spoke with a very excited tone. "I know the vehicles are used for travel, but where are they always going?"

"Work? I suppose that's where most people are going every day."

"Work? Like we work?" Ara cocked an eyebrow and sipped her tea eagerly staring up at her.

"No not exactly. People in our... realm work based on consumer products and stuff. Like, if you want to eat there has to be someone to take your order and someone to cook. Stuff like that."

"You get payed for it too." Fogstar added. "It's certainly a different place to live.

"You guys don't get payed here?" She asked. Fogstar and Ara glanced at each other.

"We don't need food or water or any of those things, if we want a house we make one or buy one. We get those gold coins distributed to us." Ara explained.

"It's not like the work we do is hard, making fog isn't exactly complicated." A cloud swelled up beside him as an example.

"Foggy gets payed more though because he's in the council." Ara smiled at him.

"Your... realm is weird."

"Plane actually, there are multiple ones. This is the *Astral* Plane." He took another sip. "It works differently in others" A golden clock chimed loudly from her left. Ara stared up at it and groaned sad they had to leave so soon.

"It was a pleasure having tea." She said as she opened the door and waved them outside.

"Thank you for your hospitality." Ara waved and closed the door, the sound of locks followed. Rebecca took one last look at the house before following Fogstar farther into the Wetlands.

Passion

Crossing the rest of the Wetlands had been sticky and wet. The longer they walked, the hotter it got, until it was almost unbearable. The landscape had changed from a swamp to a literal volcano. It wasn't actually a mountain, more of a cave. But there was lava, and it was scorching. So, so, so very hot, Rebecca couldn't breathe, it was so hot. Her hair stuck to her face with sweat. She could see Fogstar panting slightly and slowing down; Rebecca assumed he was quite tired as he had stayed up for at least a day. The ground was sizzling and oozing red hot magma they had to step over. Steam poured from small vents in the walls, red and orange crystals came pouring out of them, their spiked points reaching to the path. Rebecca looked ahead and saw the crimson-colored ground stop. A rickety old bridge connected the two ends, as she got closer she realized the bridge was made of wood and hung above boiling, bubbling lava. Rebecca hesitated to cross, but when Fogstar stepped on and continued to walk, Rebecca took a hasty step to catch up with him. She heard a bubbling noise and looked down to find a giant worm swimming in the lava. She screamed and backed up, hitting the other side of the bridge and causing it to sway dangerously.

"STOP SCREAMING!" Fogstar said as he almost tumbled off the side. "They're just Furyworms; they won't hurt you." He tried to straighten himself out as Rebecca put her weight on the other side. She looked down again at the thing below her; it looked like a rock, a cracked rock with hot magma running inside the grooves.

"What are those...?" She asked, backing away from the rope railing.

"Furyworms, they keep the place burning with passion. Do not ever touch them," Fogstar said, steadying himself once more. "And don't knock me off this bridge, please."

"Sorry…" She looked at the Furyworm as it trailed off into the distance. Ahead she saw the end of the bridge and in slightly farther what looked like a small town. "Hey, does Blaze live here?"

"No, but I do think they come here for vacation quite often." He looked ahead and kept walking. Placing their feet on solid ground and walking off away while Rebecca looked down at him, surprised.

"Astral Beings go on vacation?" Rebecca asked, quietly relieved they were on solid ground again.

"Sometimes we need a break from our duties, or want to change up the scenery," Fogstar responded. Gazing around for whatever he needed. A few extra minutes of walking ensued before they finally reached a small town of beings that Fogstar abruptly passed, leaving many gazing at them, obviously offended. Fogstar and Rebecca crossed a few other bridges, all as unsteady looking as the first, the occasional Furyworm passing under them, making Rebecca jump as it poured steamy gas onto their sides. They passed by a few other towns, all crowded with beings looking angry or flustered, most of them yelling or fighting with someone over something. Rebecca figured she should ask where they were. Fogstar responded while pushing her away from an aggressive looking snake.

"It's called Passion; they have a very interesting way of distributing population clusters and dealing with problems." He emphasized this factor by growling at another annoyed-looking shopkeeper and a woman who kept glancing at them. "It is not a dangerous place, and the beings here are not mean but... certain places do not like newcomers." As they finally made their way out of the crowded streets and steamy bridges and puddles of lava, they came across a larger town. It was hotter, and she could feel the heat burning the soles of her tennis shoes. Fogstar hopped from one foot to the other, trying to distribute heat evenly and failing as he clambered up on to the concrete sign outside of the much larger town. Its buildings made of burned clay, wood, or rock. Beings were passing, fighting over the smallest of things, burning with passion. Rebecca was gasping through the hot air to try and fill her lungs, but it was hard as the smell of smoke caused her to choke. She sat down next to Fogstar, who was also panting incessantly.

"Why does it always have to be so hot?" He said, trying to shake off the heat from his paws only to have to get back up again to get the heat off his poor tail. Rebecca smiled pitifully at him and looked around. She noticed many beings now headed to the center of the town, she didn't think much of it, but Fogstar looked curious. After a few minutes of trying to convince themselves they could walk on the blinding hot heat of the ground, they got up and set off to the center. The cave-like walls surrounded them as Fogstar tried to stay on the concrete, which didn't seem to help very much. Even the few bits of shade weren't beneficial to their cause. As they reached the considerable crowd of beings, Fogstar appeared to find a much more comfortable place to be under the overhang of a balcony. There seemed to be a crowd forming around a small stage where what looked like a hangman's pole and a noose was, and a man was standing, holding a black wolf, dripping goop. Rebecca realized what it was immediately and felt her body go numb.

It was a Nightshade follower.

A Newfound Power

The man holding up the nightshade follower had brown hair striped with red, and a dusty colored shawl draped around him. The town was cheering and throwing their fists in the air as the man tried to speak over them.

"People of Passion, we found this being stealing from a stand! It is a crime against us! We shall hang him on this day!" He lifted the wolf up by the scruff higher to show him off to the many beings now cheering louder. No more was needed to be said. He threw the wolf on the ground and told him to say his last words. Puddles of black ran down the walls and stained the streets, forming into the shapes of animals and started attacking beings. Nightshade followers sprang up all around them out of the black blots. Time stopped; first, she thought it was out of shock, but then she realized that it had actually stopped. She looked around before hearing a voice like the constant tick of a clock. She couldn't make out the words it was speaking even though she heard it loud and clear. She grabbed her head before looking down at Fogstar as time resumed. His face softened as he looked up at her; he smiled guiltily at her before bowing his head down and stepping away.

"Go ahead..." He seemed quite sad as he said this; in that sorry for you and sorry for me kind of way, but Rebecca didn't know why. She looked around; everything was turning a soft shade of white, even the Nightshade followers looked grey. Then something tackled her from behind, Rebecca tried to turn around and saw it was a large figure dripping black goop on her clothes as she struggled out of its grip. She tried to scream for Fogstar, but the words wouldn't come out. Then the white tint blinded her, and she wasn't in Passion anymore. Everything appeared made of little white triangles, mountains in the distance, small ponds of gleaming milky water, fog creeping out from under white pine trees. She heard the voice again; it said a few things she couldn't make out, and then she was back in Passion. But she wasn't wearing her clothes anymore; they were all white. Her hair wasn't tangled anymore; it had glitter in it. Her right hand felt heavy, so she looked at it and saw a shining white sword. Her head was pounding. She was standing now, and the Nightshade follower wasn't trying to attack her anymore. She looked around as all the Nightshade followers slowly stopped what they were doing and stared -- and the jaguar pounced.

Something

Rebecca felt her back hit the ground, and the air knocked out of her. She choked on the smog filling the streets. Rebecca felt tears form as if they could get the smoke and searing pain out. She swung whatever was in her right hand and felt the Nightshade follower jump off of her. It growled from somewhere in front of her. Rebecca stood up shakily and realized that there was a sword in her hand. She ran her finger on the blade, and glittering white blood fell out of the slice on her fingertip. She looked at the Nightshade follower standing beside her, his misshapen face full of terror. She looked at the blood with a frozen shock before tightening her grip and swinging at the figure.

She used the sword to stabilize herself as the Nightshade follower turned into a puddle of black goop and slushed out of town as quickly as he could. She turned to see the wolf who stood at the center of town climbing up on top of a building, shouting to the rest of them. He shouted to retreat, turning into a puddle and disappearing over the top of Passion. The rest of the Nightshade followers followed in suit. She felt her urges slow, and the weight of the sword weighed on her as everything disappeared slowly, and she fell to her knees. The force would have left bruises on anyone.

"W-what happened?" She asked as Fogstar came up with a quietly worried expression. He helped her stand up and led her over to what looked like a white house it might've been a hotel though. She couldn't make anything out as she walked up, what felt like stairs and was led through a door and put into bed. She fell asleep almost immediately; she fell into white and black dreams. White triangles and black squares, memories spilling in from the corners of her mind, some not even her own. A few beams of pink light shot out of places, and dark crystals grew out of cracks in the walls. Fog spilled out of the immature clouds, getting caught up in the beams of pink and swirling sadly. When she woke up her head hurt with a migraine, the edges of her mind fraying. She couldn't remember anything. Fogstar was asleep on the bed, snoring quietly. She got up and opened the window to the streets, which now had no Nightshade followers. She took a deep breath, which was a mistake because she ended up in a coughing fit. Fogstar woke up with a start and looked half worried and half-amused at her from behind. Once she stopped coughing, she looked behind her at Fogstar, who had changed his expression to one of self-pity and sadness she had come to expect from him. He smiled at her and beckoned her to sit down before breakfast came in, sending her stomach running in circles.

Answers

She had been stuffing her face for a few minutes now. Funny looking fruit seemed to be the best option as everything else looked like nothing she'd ever seen before, so it must taste just as bad.

 "Hey, Fogstar?" Fogstar looked up from his scroll with a curious expression as the memories of the day before caught up to her. "What happened yesterday?"

"Your Chrysalis State?" He said while calmly scribbling something down.

"My what?" He sighed and looked up at her.

"The necklace can amplify your essence to allow you to create a better suited weapon. It is only activated when in immediate danger, so when Nightshade followers are near." She gave him a confused look. "It makes you stronger and gives you a sword."

"Oh… well that's useful isn't it?" He nodded and went back to his writing. "Almost sounds like you've used it before." She twirled the little diamonds beaded chain around not looking up at Fogstar's panicked face.

"Well… no, we've never used it before." She didn't get why he was being defensive, but figured it was better not to ask. "Halo just told me to give it to you."

"You know Halo?"

"Yes, I work in her court." He said it modestly.

"Really, is that why you were chosen to come... guide me?" She didn't know what words to use to describe kidnapping. He turned away more and hesitated before nodding.

"I suppose so." They sat in silence for a few minutes, the edges of her vision cloudy with ashes.

"Fogstar?"

"Hmm?"

"Why did it choose me?" Fogstar paused and stared at whatever he was writing for a few seconds before folding it up.

"We don't know exactly. It's just supposed to choose the person it perceives best fit for the job." He looked over at her. "I'd assume it thought that was you." He had a pitiful expression on his face. He turned to lay out the map again, ignoring her. She took a deep breath, her lungs felt heavy and her arms weak. She thought she might take a nap or something to ease the burning feeling in her chest, but before she could lie down the door flew open causing its brass hinges to scream.

Arrested

Three beings paraded through the door, all wearing flaming red police uniforms, which looked quite silly on them. Fogstar didn't even seem surprised Rebecca, on the other hand, almost fell off the bed.

"YOU ARE UNDER ARREST FOR... what are they under arrest for again?" The one on the right asked as the middle one faced palmed, and the one on the left rolled his eyes.

"Un-authorized transformation in a public area." He looked over at the one on the left. "And also public endangerment." The one on the left nodded to the right, who yelled again.

"YOU ARE UNDER ARREST FOR UN-AUTHORIZED TRANSFORMATION AND PUBLIC ENDANGERMENT!" He went to grab Rebecca by the arm, but Fogstar stopped him.

"We accept these allegations; may we request a court trial?" The officer that tried to grab him looked to the middle one who nodded.

"Yes, but you're coming with me both of you!" He grabbed their arms Rebecca didn't care; she was too tired to put up a fight.

When she woke up, she was riding in a car and wasn't in Passion anymore. Fogstar was sitting next to her in the back of the vehicle, which she realized was a police car. She looked out the window finding it was dark outside now. She looked up front and saw the three officers talking quietly and messing around as they drove down the grass lined road.

"Fogstar? Why did you let them take us?" She asked. He set down what looked like a travel pamphlet for a town called Healing.

"It is much faster than walking, is it not? Plus, Nightshade's followers do not know where we are going." He said, looking out the window; they seemed to be traveling at about 40 or 50 miles per hour.

"Where are we going?" Fogstar smiled slightly before responding.

"Pursuit Tower, it's where most of the court trials and prison cells are. Of course, the cells are not in the tower; they are underground, but that is not the point." He looked up at her fondly. "Why don't you get some sl-" His ears pricked up. Rebecca didn't know why but she felt something bubble up inside her, she shoved it down and waited for Fogstar to tell her what he has scowling at. He let out a soft growl and turned his head away from the window. "So much for covering our tracks," he mumbled then curled up in a ball and told her to get some sleep though she noticed that he stayed awake. After a few minutes of trying, she found she couldn't fall asleep, with the sound of the rumbling engine and the imminent threat of Nightshade followers. Instead, she just looked out the window, watching passing lights swirl by and the flashes of beings clambering through the night. A few times she saw what looked like a small drop of black goop splatter on the window but could never make them out for long enough to decipher whether or not they were Nightshade followers. She looked out the window, feeling nostalgic. The roads lined with dead bushes looked like the desert road trips her family would take. Her thoughts turned to her parents and her life on Earth. Were they even looking for her? They must be at least a little worried, right? They had to at least be trying to find her, though, she didn't want to go home, at least not until Nightshade was defeated and the Astral Plane saved. Knowing Fogstar wasn't asleep, it certainly took a long time before he decided to point out she wasn't sleeping. When he finally did, he looked up at her again with a knowing face.

"Sorry... can't sleep." She looked out the window as Fogstar nodded and turned back around to look out the window. "Do you think my parents are looking for me?" He sat up and looked at her before they both said sorry at the same time. "No, you wouldn't know, sorry for asking."

"No, it's my fault I should know and answer your questions." They both looked away, Rebecca laughed, and Fogstar smiled looking out the window again before facing her. "You really should go to sleep." She grinned and turned back to the window. It only took a few seconds before she fell asleep against the car window drifting into more dreams of swirling lights and black shadows covering them, dark clouds swirling over the black sky. Lights getting dimmer and dimmer until all she could see was a void. She woke up a few times, once she finally saw the tower, or at least what she thought it was. She couldn't get a good view because it was so dark, but she could see blue and red lights spinning at the top about 500 feet in the air. A line of cars that looked exactly like the one she was in stretched out in front of them for what seemed like miles before going into a hole where she thought the base of the tower should be. She thought for a few seconds that she was still dreaming until Fogstar sighed and sat back down impatiently. The drivers leaned back in their seats to prepare for the long line of traffic in front of them. She decided to go back to sleep, as it would take a while. Tomorrow would be an exhausting day.

Waiting

When she woke up again, she heard sirens and saw a girl with a spiky ponytail running as fast as she could past them towards the tower, which, now that it was light outside, could be seen clearly. It had black and white checkered walls and red and blue sirens on top of it hundreds feet in the air. The line of traffic had significantly shortened since last night as they were only a few cars ahead of them before the hole in the wall leading into a parking garage type place. Once they finally got inside and parked, the officers said their goodbyes and went separate ways. The 'smarter' one led them to a rather large waiting room. They sat down in between a lizard looking man wearing a suit and top hat, two insect wings folded behind him, and a man with a blue and purple planet head. His oversized grey t-shirt and blue jeans looked more comforting than the lizard man's annoyed expression, so she took her chances with the planet instead.

"Hi, what are you here for?" Rebecca said, looking over at him.

"Oh! Hello!" From the tone of his voice, she guessed he smiled at her. "My name's Leaf, public speaking violations..." He sighed dramatically, like it shouldn't have been as big a deal as it was.

"I'm Rebecca, what did you say to get arrested for public speaking?" She asked before shaking his hand. She thought he laughed, but without a mouth, she couldn't tell.

"Oh, some Nightshade followers attacking Ease. I was there on vacation with my girlfriend." He said, glancing over at the even more annoyed expression on the lizard man's face.

"Oh… uh…" She glanced down at Fogstar, who looked up at her and muttered.

"They're going to follow us everywhere. We made sure to pick towns that could deal with Nightshade attacks." Leaf kicked his legs innocently staring at the ceiling.

"I haven't seen her in days, I just hope she's alright…" Leaf said, dropping his shoulders sadly.

"What were you doing in Ease, besides vacation?"

"Oh nothing, or at least nothing I was aware of. We like the tea there, and the people. It's so relaxed you know? And Static says she likes the busy streets for some reason. We got a nice rented apartment north of Centre."

"That sounds lovely I hope you see her again soon." Rebecca turned her gaze over to the empty reception counter. A tiny girl who looked about 6 popped up wearing a gigantic pink bow, her black hair tied up in pigtails. She started calling out numbers.

"42-A, 42-A?" She sang out as the lizard man got up, rolling his eyes, his hands in his pockets. Next to him sat a small egg shaped man with a terrified look on his face.

"MisterEmeraldyouareunderarrestforbreakingandenteringas wellasbeingheadofacriminalparty.Yourtrialwillbeheldonfloorf ortytwofirstdooronyourright." She smiled and handed him a ticket. She talked very, very fast, so fast that Rebecca couldn't make out half of what she said. The little egg man jumped when his number got called, walking up to the counter, shaking uncontrollably.

"Sir,youaskedforacourtmeetingafterbeingcorneredbyabeing inacloak,whatdidsheaskyouagain?" She asked him.

"Uh... S-she asked w-where the P-planetarium was..." He grabbed his ticket and stepped into the elevator. Leaf was 'biting' his nails worriedly.

"What's the Planetarium?" Rebecca whispered to Fogstar, who was sitting at her feet.

"It is the housing area for all planet beings." He gestured to Leaf as the little girl called out another number.

"44-F, 44-F?"

"That's us." Fogstar got up and walked over to the counter.

"Courttrialforunauthorizedchangesequenceandpublic endangerment.Yourtrialwillbeheldonfloorfortyfour,sixthdoor onyourleft." She handed them a ticket, and they stepped into the elevator with good luck wishes by both Leaf and the receptionist. She had a feeling they would need it. The inside of the elevator was sleek and classy, as Fogstar pressed button 44 under the label of 'courtroom.'

"Why would anyone want to attack the Planetarium?" Fogstar looked around and then up at her.

"I do not know, he said they were looking for someone, maybe they're not trying to attack just trying to..." Fogstar cut himself off, but Rebecca knew exactly what he was going to say.

"Kidnap someone?" He nodded slowly before turning to face the door of the elevator in suspense of the trial. They didn't talk about it after that, not even after the court trial.

Court

The elevator went up and up, the little yellow light counting the numbers. Fogstar seemed a little nervous as he sat down looking at the numbers though Rebecca figured it was just her. After all, what was there about to be worried? There were no Nightshade followers here, and with Fogstar's skills in communication, how could they lose? They were on floor 23 before Rebecca could process it.

24, 25, 26, 27, 2-

"You're going to be the defendant; I hope I don't have to be your defense." Fogstar said with a pained expression as they reached floor 28. Rebecca paused for a moment.

29, 30, 31, 32, 3-

"I don't really know how courts work Fogstar." She stared down at him, his ears went down.

"That's alright just...just tell the truth." He took a deep breath as they reached forty.

37, 38, 39, 4-

"So what do you want me to do?" She asked.

Fogstar sighed, "Just tell the truth."

41, 42, 43, 44.

The elevator doors opened slowly, they both hesitated, glancing at each other before stepping out warily and walking down the hall to the sixth door on their left. Inside was a large room, a wooden stand at the back and two more facing each other in front of it. The walls closed in around them with black screens covering the jury members. They all had white uniforms with a scale badge. They all went silent when Rebecca and Fogstar entered the room. Two of the stands were filled, the one in the back with a woman in her late thirties. Her hair was black but had been starting to grey. Her suit and tie fit but not the large blindfold covering what little of a face she had. The podium on her right had a man in a very fancy suit, black with grey pinstripes and white lace around his collar and wrists. His grey hair tied back into a small ponytail.

"Rebecca Miller?" The woman at the front asked. She assumed she was the judge. Fogstar leaned in to whisper.

"You can only answer to her in words she can't see."

"What's the point of being a judge if you can't see?" Fogstar glanced at her and sighed. He gave a small nod to the jury stand and climbed up the small steps to an open seat. He pulled out a little "witness" card and placed it in front of him. He glared at the empty stand before resorting to silent praying.

"Yes, I am Rebecca Miller." That was, in fact, her name. For some reason the other man wouldn't make eye contact with her.

"If Innocence is late we will have to resort to having your traveling partner defend you," the judge said gesturing to Fogstar. Now she knew what he was so worked up about.

"Guilt will be the prosecution, he may call witness to anyone he'd like. Do you understand Miller?"

"Yes?" She thought she knew how courts worked, she was wrong.

"Good." A door opened from behind and another man rushed out holding a stack of papers.

"Sorry Justice." He heaved the things onto his desk. "That was a long trial." His hair curled to rest right below his ears, streaks of blond glinted from certain hairs. His smile was brighter than a diamond as he turned to Guilt and then filed through his papers.

"And Innocence will be the defense, I understand Mi-"

"Yes." She cut him off, growing impatient.

"Then we may begin." Justice lifted her hands equal to her head and waited. Guilt and Innocence both looked at her waiting for her to turn to one of them. She made eye contact with Guilt first, his black eyes piercing her soul. She blinked a few times before looking away. Innocence's yellow stained eyes looked like glass. She made a curious expression before looking away. They whispered something to Justice in turn she gave them both a look before sighing and reaching for her blindfold. Everyone, including Fogstar, shielded their eyes from her. She pulled down the piece of fabric to reveal pale, pale blue... she wouldn't exactly call them eyes. More like spheres inside her head. A few seconds later she pulled the thing back up in disgust.

"Innocent of charges," she muttered, turning to Guilt who shrugged.

"What's going on again?" Rebecca didn't like whatever they were doing. They weren't treating her like person.

"I believe we are done here." Guilt flipped his papers, letting his eyes fall over her. "I expect to see you again."

They were ushered out of the room after that. They sat in the waiting room for an hour or two, biding time and making conversation before a jury member came out of the elevator and handed them a few papers. Fogstar told her to put them away. She nodded and told them they were free to go, a car was waiting outside. It was sunset when she stepped outside where amber light was cascading down the side of the tower.

"Well that went better than expected," Fogstar smiled. She wanted to ask questions but didn't think she liked the people enough to dignify them Fogstar's response.

Road

It was night by the time they got to the car. As they were driving, rain battered down on the window steadily. Fogstar smiled a bit as he looked out the window, which Rebecca thought was weird for him, but she knew why and was grinning too. Ara was checking in on them; it was nice to know someone cared. But as that thought branched out it got sadder, what was her mother doing right now, her brother? Her family had never been that close, her dad working in the army and Rebecca having a teenage brother. But they had to have at least called the police right? They had to have at least tried looking for her. Fogstar looked at her awkwardly; again, he sighed and turned to her.

"You know you will get back soon..."

"But what if I don't?" Her voice choked on the last part. "You said it yourself, I might not get home, whether that is because I can't leave the Astral Plane or..." He stared at her, she knew he regretted something when he looked at her; she didn't know what though. He was about to answer with some hope speech that he looked like he would dread, but then his ears perked up, and his expression dropped.

"Move the car off the road."

"Why?" Their driver looked at them, suspiciously from behind the seat.

"Because I said so. MOVE!" The car swerved off the road into a tree, the driver didn't do that. Black swirled around them Rebecca knew what was going on immediately. She hadn't used her Chrysalis form since Passion, but she focused hard. Energy poured out of her, and she grabbed hold of it, when she opened her eyes she was back in the white abyss, the voice was back too.

"Go a-head, sa-vior..." She could finally understand that stupid clock voice, he spoke like every syllable was the tick of a clock. Then she was back to the Astral Plane as it faded back to time, she drew her sword and opened the car door before lunging at the nearest Nightshade follower. His face of terror was priceless. She swung and hit his arm as he reared back and then pounced at her again. She turned and struck his chest; she looked away before seeing the result of that action. She leaped at another one and felt it scratch her face. Fogstar was hissing and fighting the smaller beings; blood was running down his leg. She felt clawing on her leg and kicked off a small black mass. Her hair felt damp, and the air was thick with blood and goop.

She didn't like it. She slashed at another being with her sword, knocking it to the ground.

Faulty

She kept fighting, it got tiring after a while, but they just kept coming. It didn't seem like the best option right now, but there wasn't anywhere else to go. She shook another Nightshade follower off her other foot and slashed at a humanoid being that was moving towards her. Apparently, they came prepared this time; they knew she could use her Chrysalis form now. Dark trees swirled around them, blocking any chance of escape they might get. The sky was dark and foggy, she wondered if that was Fogstar's fault. She lunged at another being, come to think of it, their numbers were decreasing. Less and less of them were coming back, and black goop filled the forest floor where they stood. It became sort of a trance to hit them over and over again. Then at some point most of Nightshade's followers were no more. The four that were still there took notice of the situation and ran the other way. She was pretty grateful that it was over. She looked over at the car, the roof bent with paws and hands of all sorts, and a door pulled off its hinges and thrown to the ground. Rebecca saw the driver knocked out, she felt sorry for him. She turned around to look at Fogstar instead.

"Will he be ok?" she asked. She had stopped looking at Fogstar, who was sitting in a clearing of the goop licking the many, many, *many* gashes that decorated his fur, again.

"What?" Fogstar glanced at her quizzically.

 "Will he be okay?" She thrust a finger over her shoulder to point at the car.

"Oh, yes. Someone will find him sooner or later." She nodded before gazing down at Fogstar again.

"Will you be okay?" She asked, but she already knew the answer and looked down the road into the darkness. "Where do we go?"

"Um…" Fogstar looked around and sighed. "They know where we are…"

"And we don't?"

"No, I know where we are, but… we can't stay here and…" Rebecca looked at him worriedly, was there nowhere to go? No shelter? Would they have to sleep in the forest? "We need to rest, would you be able to fight by tomorrow?"

"Yeah…why?" She eyed him suspiciously. He looked doubtful.

"Smokescreen."

Smokescreen

Rebecca and Fogstar had been walking through the forest for 15 minutes or so when she asked, "But, didn't you say he is bad?"

"Working with Nightshade." Fogstar was not happy with what he was suggesting, but there seemed to be no choice.

"WORKING WITH NIGHTSHADE?"

"I know it's not the best option, but it's our *only* option." It was almost dawn; the way the 'sun' lit up the Astral Plane and danced off the leaves made her feel all warm and fuzzy inside. White clouds filled the yellow tinged sky, and fresh air filled her lungs. She loved it, but now they were approaching a vast hill of grey grass, filled with houses, the bottom wasn't as covered and had a substantial black wooden house in the center. Fogstar sighed and turned to her, "This is Mt. Fatal..."

"Well, I can guess who lives here..." She looked around at the grey houses and odd substances pouring out of chimneys on the top of slanted roofs. One house, in particular, caught her eye, it was sleek and light grey, a black river flew beside it. It looked like it was made out of slate.

"There..." Fogstar pointed to the house at which she was looking.

"Of course," She said.

"Okay, listen you need not give him your name. The more he trusts you, the better, so try to pretend you trust him. Okay?"

"Yes?" She didn't know how to do that, but that didn't matter now. They walked along the forest floor, and as soon as she stepped onto the grass she felt the air fill with smoke and death, her insides turned out, and Rebecca felt like she was going to throw up. Fogstar looked the same way. They knocked on the door, which was as hard as a rock, and it swung open almost immediately.

"I told you, Oracle, you come back here one more time, shouting about that stupid pro- oh…" A cat looked up at them, he looked surprised. His fur was darker than Fogstar's, and his paws detailed with smoke and ashes. He was probably Smokescreen. For a being working with Nightshade, he wasn't as -- black goop monster as she expected. He had invited them in almost immediately and had made a kettle of vision tea for them. Fogstar kept throwing looks at him from the couch on which they were sitting. The house decorated with all kinds of burnable items. He had a fireplace covered in stones and what looked like a table full of old pictures. The walls were slate, and his kitchen, like every being's, was small and compact. The central spot was the living room; a wooden door was off to the side. She guessed it led to his bedroom.

"Lovely house…" She said, looking over awkwardly at Smokescreen as he poured tea into cups.

"Thank you." He nodded and then looked up at them teasingly. "I bought it from a friend of his." He gestured towards Fogstar, who seemed to be disgusted at the fact that Smokescreen had even indirectly mentioned him. "So why did you come here?" He handed her a cup, she took it and nodded thankfully. Fogstar just glared at him until he set it down.

"Well, we got attacked, and there was nowhere else to go, it was Fogstar's idea," Rebecca said, Smokescreen stopped dead in his tracks to look at Fogstar.

"You came here… on your own terms?" Smokescreen asked as Fogstar jolted up.

"Didn't you hear what she said? No, we were attacked by Nightshade followers and had no choice. As if I'd ever come back here because I wanted to." Fogstar growled at him from the corner as Smokescreen set a cup on the table for himself.

"Okay, what happened between you two?" Rebecca whispered to Fogstar as Smokescreen walked back to the kitchen and set down the kettle.

"Nothing you need to know about." Just as Fogstar had finished his sentence, Smokescreen turned to look at him.

"Things that Foggy will refrain from talking about to you. A tragedy you probably should know about, but of course he won't mention," Smokescreen said. Apparently he had heard them. Fogstar's eye drifted for a split second, and then he burst out with rage.

"You are not allowed to bring that up! It was your fault we almost got killed here last time!" Fogstar almost knocked over his tea while saying this.

"I would never have done anything to hurt Abbigail! In fact I didn't. How many times do I have to tell you? I didn't bring those Nightshade followers here! You must believe me because you brought another Savoir here," Smokescreen shouted. Fogstar looked at him surprised before angrily whispering at him.

"I haven't told her yet..."

"And knowing you, you never will!" Smokescreen turned away and walked back to the kitchen to do whatever he was doing, "You can stay the night."

Secrets

"So... who's Abbigail?" Rebecca asked as they entered the wooden door that led off to a stone hallway. Two doors branched off, and by the smoke seeping out from under one, that was not their room.

"No one..." He seemed a little upset, but by the amount of arguing in this house, that was probably why. It kinda looked like seeing his brother again was the worst decision of his life, which it probably was.

"Did she mean something to you?" Fogstar stopped dead in his tracks and then looked down.

"No..." She could tell he was lying, but by the crack in his voice, she knew it must have been a touchy subject. Fogstar opened the door for her, and she entered a small room with a queen-sized bed draped with grey silk and fluffy black pillows. Smoky clouds were floating above her head and a white vase with a dead flower in it. It smelled like smoke and death; she scrunched up her nose and sat down on the bed. She tried to remember what Smokescreen had said, but the words just floated around in her head with empty meaning... Fogstar sat down in a corner and pulled a map and a red pen out of a fog cloud. She wouldn't get answers from him even if she tried. She figured that they would spend the rest of the day in silence, but Smokescreen came in a few times to bring, or to make sure they hadn't left or something... she wouldn't be surprised if that had happened once. She had looked around the room for something to do, but all she could see were books in an unknown language and a black sky outside her window. Once Fogstar had finished tracking where they had gone, he put everything back and turned to her slowly.

"I know you think that Smokescreen is nice, I thought that too, but we almost died here because we trusted him. I will never make that mistake again, and I don't care how many friends I lose." He jumped up onto the bed and rested his head on his paws to stare out the window with her.

"You sound like you hate your brother a lot," she said while refraining from looking at him. Fogstar paused for a second.

"I don't hate him." He took a deep breath staring out the window. "I just don't trust him anymore."

Writing back

Rebecca and Fogstar had been staring out the window for what felt like forever when Rebecca remembered that she needed to write back to someone.

"Hey, do you have any scrolls?" Fogstar looked up at her curiously; she didn't think anyone had ever asked that.

"Sure… here" A fog cloud formed next to him, and he pulled out a yellowed piece of paper rolled into a cylinder. He handed it to her along with a fancy black fountain pen. She unrolled the scroll and started writing back to Halo,

Hello Halo, my name is Rebecca, but you probably know that already…

She rolled up the scroll, and Fogstar handed her a red stamp thing. She didn't know what to do with it, so she just looked at it. Then she turned to Fogstar, who seemed to see the problem and rolled his eyes.

"Really? You don't know how to use these?" She shook her head and watched as he tied a scratchy string around the scroll and stamped a red seal on the bow. It looked a bit like her necklace, which she made sure to check before asking.

"How are we going to send this?"

"Next town over has a postal station…" Fogstar looked torn. She didn't understand why but it seemed like it had something to do with Abbigail… who appeared to be brought up more often here than anywhere else in the whole Astral Plane. She nodded and looked out the window again, "Hey! Is it darker outside than usual?" Fogstar's ears pressed back, and he growled.

Black Clouds

Outside of the window, the sky curled in with black clouds, and she didn't know what that meant until a few seconds later when black sludge splattered the window and two orange eyes popped out. They looked through the window for a few seconds before spotting them and smiled; it turned around and screeched. Probably the worst sound she had ever heard. Fogstar growled before turning around and shoving a book in one of his fog clouds.

"Um, Fogstar?" The window was starting to crack as three piles of goop pounded on the glass.

"I know, I know...," He filed around for a second and then shoved a few papers in another cloud. "Okay, let's go."

They burst through the door and ran through the hall into the kitchen where Smokescreen was tackled by another of Nightshades' followers. Doubt filled her mind before she realized that Fogstar had already run for the door. She turned around, and then she faded into the white landscape of, well, wherever she went when she transformed. The voice didn't say anything; she was just pushed out with a sword in her hand and glitter in her hair. A Nightshade follower tackled her from behind; she fell over on her side swinging to get him off. Her vision clouded with black as they swarmed above her and droplets of their black body parts dripped onto her. She raised her sword and cut through a few of them balancing herself and stumbling to fend off the rest of the Nightshade followers around her. She heard Smokescreen's coughing through the hissing and screeching. As she killed the last of the followers she finally spotted him forming clouds of smoke to try and avoid being tackled. She ran over and swung at the Nightshade follower that was about to kill Smokescreen. He looked up at her, thankful, and slightly confused; she didn't think anyone had ever saved him before.

"WHAT ARE YOU DOING?" Fogstar's words only just made it to her ears through all the weird sounds the black puddles were making. She grabbed Smokescreen and adjusted her sword in her hand before bolting across the paved slate to the door. She set Smokescreen down and turned to look at Fogstar, who was looking up at her, confused.

"You have to get out of here," Smokescreen said, looking around as the Nightshade follower frenzy was taking over his house.

"I agree," Fogstar said, moving a little further towards the wall.

"Go for the door, I'll make sure to distract them. I know you hate me Foggy but I promise you I never called those Nightshade followers here. I'd never hurt my little brother, much less a Savior, and I don't care if you won't believe that. If I don't…" He turned to look at the Nightshade followers. "Tell Mistral I love her. Now, go–" Fogstar tried to say something but the words just wouldn't come out. She saw what looked like tears form but couldn't tell for sure. Without another word they opened the door and ran as fast as they could far, far from Mt. Fatal and into the black smoke swirling up through the trees.

Pathway

The landscape around them had changed immensely since leaving Smokescreen's house. The black and green leaves had changed to a brighter lighter color and, just recently, pink. The clouds had faded back to white, and they seemed even fluffier. However, the most important thing that changed was Fogstar's attitude. He was furious at himself for Smokescreen, but as they had crossed, what looked like a border to a new town he seemed to get ...scared? It was hard to read his expression now, but Rebecca tried to pay attention to other things, like the actual sunlight beating down on her face and the beautiful light surrounding the forest or the perfectly paved path of brown gravel on which they were walking. She took a deep breath and stretched her arms, they were a bit sore from swinging her sword, but she didn't mind. Fogstar looked up at her while she looked fondly up at the cherry blossoms falling from the trees.

"She loved them too..." Fogstar whispered just as Rebecca turned around to look at him curiously. "Um, I mean, *I* love them..." He cleared his throat and looked back down at his paws.

"You've been here before?" She decided to change the subject.

"Yes... It's a lovely town, the people too." He looked up at her, and they started an actual conversation, which they hadn't done in two days. They talked about what to expect inside the next town, which was called Nostalgia. She thought it was a nice name and Fogstar agreed then voiced the next point. They both might be thinking about other things than the present and or future. Nostalgia only gave memories from the past and sometimes the present. Fogstar kept bringing up a 'she' in the conversation and then denying it; maybe the effects of Nostalgia were already kicking in for him. But it didn't matter because Rebecca knew that Fogstar would never spill any of his secrets to her.

"Anyhow," he continued, "I will find us a place to stay for the night. But after that may I leave you alone for a day?" He looked up at her pleadingly.

"What? Well..." She looked around. "Sure, why not? Why? What do you need to do?" Fogstar stopped and tried to think of an excuse. It didn't seem like he could so she just shook it off and let him lead her through a yellowed, cracked archway reading, Welcome to Nostalgia.

Nostalgia

As they walked through the archway, beings seemed to recognize Fogstar, they spoke to him and waved, and some of them even looked like they empathized with him. She knew he had been here before, but wow, he made an impact. Rebecca looked down at him as he walked silently through the town. Her mind followed each day slowly; she thought of her Mom, and the cake she made for her 6th birthday. Her Dad and how happy they all were when we came home for Christmas. Her brother and how he had scolded her about Clara. She thought about Dex and how he introduced Becky to her for the first time. About Connor playing spin the bottle at one of the popular kid's parties a year before and the time Grayson acted extremely suspiciously when asked why he looked like he been up all night crying. She thought about meeting Fogstar for the first time… The streets around her were a blur but she could see yellowed buildings stacked on top of one another and cherry trees with their leaves falling to the ground. She snapped out of her trance and remembered she needed to send the letter to Halo. Fogstar pointed her to a mailbox, and she slipped the note inside. Soon they came upon a building reaching up to the clouds; there was a sign that had said, *Present Hotel, for all your new thoughts.* So she looked up at the hotels' many balconies with loopy white railing. The windows were stained white, and hints of pink stuck out in streaks along the surface of the walls. Fogstar and Rebecca walked inside to find the same beauty. Fogstar walked over to the front desk, made of marble. The woman sitting there was holding a phone and talking into it when she noticed them; she held up a finger and smiled.

"Yes, Drav, I have your reservation… of course… no problem… thank you!" She put down the phone and rolled the pink seat she was sitting in over to the counter. "Hello, Fogstar, same room as always? Who's this?" She looked at Rebecca.

"That's confidential thanks, Marty." He grabbed the door keys she had put on the counter and headed to the elevator. Marty looked at Fogstar pitifully but let him go on his way. The elevator took them up a few floors and opened to a hallway with marble floors. Fogstar turned to room 44 and opened the door to an ivory carpeted room. A large window with a balcony was on her right. The pink curtains swayed in the sunlight casting a rose-colored beam that illuminated the walls. The bed stood in the center of the room with cream-colored sheets, fairy lights hung from the ceiling, even though they were turned off the effect was still there. A bouquet of pink and white lilies floated through the door and set down on a small table, Fogstar smiled slightly and went to bed, and Rebecca did too

Grave

Rebecca opened her eyes slowly; sunlight poured through the window encasing the room in a golden embrace. She sat up and rubbed her eyes, then looking around, she noticed that Fogstar wasn't there. A quick bolt of fear ran up her spine as she wondered where he had gone. Rebecca headed to the elevator where she noticed that the bouquet of lilies on the table was gone. Rebecca pressed the ground floor button and watched the numbers count down. Marty was still at the counter typing on a computer. She looked up at Rebecca for a second and then went back to whatever she was working on.

"Hey, did you see where Fogstar went?" she asked. Marty looked up at her fully now.

"He went up to that hill he always goes to. He didn't tell you?"

"He asked if he could leave me alone for a while, why?"

"Well you know the Savoir and all..." Marty went back to typing, Rebecca was very confused.

"Why does he go up there?"

"It's where they buried... well not buried but, they put a grave up there. He's been going for 100 years straight. The poor guy... I really feel sorry for him..." Marty took a sip from her pink coffee cup.

"Grave? Someone died?" Rebecca felt slightly betrayed at not being told this very important fact. Did someone actually die? Who?

"Um, yeah? First Nightshade War, everybody knows that. But you're not just "anybody" are you? He didn't tell you about it?"

"There was a Nightshade war before this?" Rebecca couldn't believe no one had shared this with her before.

"Of course, well why don't you think he hasn't killed you yet? If he wasn't trapped he would've probably slit your throat while you were sleeping."

What did that mean? There was another Savoir before her? No, Fogstar had made it very clear she was the only one. She was supposed to be the only one. But you can't exactly fight Nightshade without a Savoir, can you? Why had he lied? "There was another Savoir… Why didn't I… her name wouldn't have happened to be Abbigail was it?"

"I think it was something like that, yeah." Marty gave her some poorly explained directions and watched as Rebecca ran out the door. It was like she was watching a bad television drama.

The morning fog stung her eyes as she spotted the place, a grassy hill with cherry trees dotted on top. It didn't look like there was any fencing so she climbed up the walkway and prepared herself to be let down by a history lesson.

Confession

Rebecca hid behind the trunk of a huge dark cherry tree in the middle of pink grass and leaves beside the huddled figure of Fogstar. The bouquet of lilies lying in front of a modest gravestone engraved with words of thanks. Rebecca didn't want to startle him so she just stood there for a second watching. Finally, she stepped out from behind the tree. Fogstar saw her but didn't seem to move. The regret that filled his face told her enough though.

"I'm sorry..." Rebecca said sitting down next to him. He sniffled up the tears that had matted down his fur. "What happened?" He furrowed his eyebrows angrily.

"I didn't want you to come here," he said looking away from her.

"I'm sorry but I heard about another Savoir and I-"

"I didn't want you to come here," he was angry now. Rebecca didn't realize he could be defensive but it made some sense. He wouldn't want to talk about something like death, though he needed to because she wanted to know what had happened. "Please go away." Even as he said it he knew that wouldn't work.

"No. What happened?" She didn't know how to get Fogstar to talk to her. She didn't understand why she hadn't seen it sooner, there were so many signs. But how was she supposed to know there had been another Savior? She thought she was the only one, one of a kind for once in her life. He didn't even look at her, he just sat there. He looked on the verge of tears. "Fogstar?"

"You want to know what happened." His voice was edged with pain.

"Of course I do! That's what I've been asking."

"Fine, you know what? 100 years ago we had a war with Nightshade and we needed a Savoir. So we got Abbigail and she was great. She was amazing. Did everything she was supposed to, and then when we made it to Halo's tower Nightshade attacked us. When we couldn't defeat him she…" He trailed off losing the angry tone while thinking about whatever happened. Fog swirled around them and Rebecca wasn't in Nostalgia anymore. The sun beat down on her open arms and the dry ground was littered with the remains of Nightshade followers. They were stuck to the soles of her shoes. She turned around to see the whole of the Astral Plane fighting Nightshade followers. A pink beam bolted up into the clouds. Everyone turned to look at it. The fog faded away and she was back in Nostalgia staring at Fogstar who seemed to be surprised he had done that. Or maybe it was reliving such a terrible memory that caused the look of shock.

"She died, I know that, but was she killed or…?" Fogstar couldn't keep it up any longer and began sobbing towards the ground. Rebecca reached for him but gave up a few seconds later. He didn't look like he wanted a hug, he just wanted to cry. She didn't understand that about people.

"She knew she couldn't defeat him so she gave herself up to imprison him… I didn't want to tell you." A brief moment of hesitation passed before he choked out his second line. "I thought you would be mad at me."

"Well… You should've told me before, and then we wouldn't have to have this kind of a conversation," she said matter of factly. He turned away guiltily.

"I thought you would be scared if I told you the last Savior died."

"Yeah…" She thought about it for a second. She knew she might die while fighting Nightshade but the reality of it finally hit her. She might die like Abbigail, or maybe not. She believed she was better than her.

"I'm sorry." Fogstar looked over at the gravestone like he had betrayed it then looked over at Rebecca again.

"Thank you for apologizing," Rebecca smiled. "That's all that happened? Just a war?"

"Yes, just a war. When she died everybody was so… sad, they didn't even know her. They didn't deserve to be sad when we had just won the war. It was bittersweet and worse *they* all got comfort and help. They didn't even know her. To make it even worse I had to sit in a courtroom and write down what had happened over and over again until my head hurt so much I had to stop." The sun fell below the crest of the hill it was getting steadily darker and darker. Rebecca suggested going back to the hotel; Fogstar stared at the bouquet but ended up going with her as the sun left Nostalgia.

Honesty

They reached the hotel after about 15 minutes of walking. Fogstar rushed them up the elevator away from Marty who looked worried about him. The hotel room looked very different in the moonlight. Fogstar curled up on the bed and stared at her.

"Yes?"

"Nothing..." he said but he didn't look away. "You look like her sometimes." Rebecca didn't like that. She hated being compared to someone weak enough to sacrifice themselves; she went to sit down next to Fogstar.

"How long do 100 years feel to the people here?" Rebecca asked.

"About a year your time." It was less than Rebecca thought it would be. She had expected more like a decade or something. "It feels like it was yesterday though... or last month maybe," Fogstar mumbled looking sad again. She didn't want him to cry. She wanted to change the subject but couldn't find anything different to talk about so they sat in silence for a while

 "I guess everyone in the Astral Plane knows she's dead," Rebecca observed.

"Yes, you can imagine how many beings gave her flowers in the beginning." His eyes were blurry as he stared at the floor.

"Do you ever talk about her?" Rebecca knew the answer but figured she needed to be sure. If he didn't talk about her it would be a good thing, she wouldn't have to bring her up since it made him so sad. Though that wasn't exactly the main reason she didn't like talking about her.

"No," he thought he needed to explain it. "The others need someone to ground them and I don't think they would understand."

"I don't understand either, they are immature next to you," she said. He looked like he had wanted to hear something else. "Something that happened a year ago you should be over it by now, right?"

"It doesn't feel that way," his breath was shaky, he was holding in those tears like the world depended on it.

"Well, I don't think it would be a good idea to talk to them about it," she said. He nodded assured of something in his head. "I'm here for you though; of course I still think it's a bit silly but..." she trailed off. She didn't want to open herself up to talking about Abbigail, but she figured it would make Fogstar trust her more. He looked up at her with a thankful smile.

 "You're a good friend you know that?" Of course, she did but it was nice to know he thought that about her.

"Yeah, you're a good friend too," she said. He shook his head sadly.

"No, I haven't done anything for you. Is there anything you want me to do?" She thought for a second, he did owe her something for this, but she decided he had already given her everything she needed.

"No, I have everything I could want right here." She patted his head and climbed under the sheet. Fogstar sat at the end of the bed for a few moments, thinking about something, before following her. It only took a few minutes for her to fall asleep, seeing as the wind was blowing and there wasn't anything to worry about. She heard Fogstar whisper a thank you before being carried off to dreamland. She didn't take the time to consider what he was saying thank you for, she was far too tired for that.

Silence

The next day Rebecca got up before Fogstar, the curtains were blowing softly into the room, and the sun was pouring through the open windows. Fogstar was still fast asleep on the bed; his back was rising and falling slowly, he seemed to be having pleasant dreams. Rebecca walked out onto the ivory-colored balcony and looked down at the streets below. She listened in on the sound of everyone walking peacefully along the streets in the beautiful trance of the past. She thought it was silly, always thinking of the past, I mean wouldn't you want to live in the present? This thought continued for a while before she heard Fogstar wake up behind her. When she stepped back inside the room, she knew they had to leave today. But it seemed like the worst time to go, they were safe here. She assumed that Nightshade's followers were sick and tired of getting beaten by her and Fogstar. Maybe they would finally stop attacking and retreat to where ever they came. Then again, they didn't seem like the types to give up on a kill. Fogstar opened the elevator for them and pressed the button to the ground floor. Marty checked them out and gave Fogstar a look of pity, luckily he didn't see. The clouds were still fluffy and white, and the streets lit with lanterns. Beings stayed off the roads for the most part, and it was a clear path out of Nostalgia. They walked under another beige arch of wood and Rebecca felt the sense of Nostalgia drip off of her. As the two of them walked away in silence the scenery changed from the beautiful aesthetic of Nostalgia to a quiet wood. The clouds were orange, and the trees were dark and thick. The world was silent here, and before Rebecca could ask where they were, a sign appeared from around a corner saying, **Silent Forest**, *No talking.*

Rebecca thought it was funny and laughed, but no sound came out. Fogstar seemed perfectly fine without noise as the birds flying through the trees made no sound, and when the wind blew leaves didn't rattle or shake. It was like someone pressed mute on the world, and Rebecca couldn't stand it. She wanted to get out of here as soon as possible, which was convenient because just then, the world turned back on, and the ground got wet and soggy. The trees drooped over as the leaves fell off slowly. She thought that it was a swamp, but there was an odd sense of insanity that filled the air.

"I don't think we should be here..." Fogstar said just as a hand covered Rebecca's mouth, and they were in darkness.

Psycho

When Rebecca opened her eyes, they burned. She had to cough a few times before she tried to stand up, she found couldn't. Ropes tied her to a thick wooden post. She attempted to wriggle her way out of. She heard a few noises muffled in the background. As she looked around, she realized she was in a house, more like a cabin. The cabin was built of dark wood, and the smell of the swampy ground filled the air. A door creaked from behind her; she heard a few voices arguing about something.

"We have to do something with her." She heard a very hoarse and high pitched voice creak. It sounded like a child that had been screaming for a while.

"Well, what do we do? We can't kill her..." Another more scared voice asked.

"Why not? We could kill her! It would make for a wonderful dinner." A third voice suggested from behind the pole she was tied to.

"No, you can't kill her." Fogstar's voice responded. He walked out from behind the post and flashed her a look before glancing up at the three figures walking out. They were all glaring at her. There was a floating eyeball with giant lilac wings that suspended him in the air, a very tall woman in a long purple cloak with wavy black spirals all over it and a clock head, which would sometimes turn back a few minutes. Lastly, a tiny child stood in a long, clawed, straight jacket.

"Why not, Foggy?" The clock asked, looking at him with a flash of hatred in her black eyes.

"I don't think she would taste that good anyway…" The child added, poking her in the arm and looking at her disgustedly. Fogstar looked like he wanted her to stop but he didn't dare touch her.

"Hmmm, you said you found her in the forest and… what was it again?" The eye asked, flapping his wings a few more times to keep him in the air.

"She was all bloodied and hurt so I decided I would get her help. This was the first place I saw," Fogstar replied. Rebecca nodded silently as the clock walked up to her and bent down to look her in the eyes.

"We should introduce ourselves!" The child said, causing the clock to back up slightly. "This is Pupil," she pointed at the eye who looked like he would've waved if he had arms, "and this is Anomily," she pointed at the clock who puffed up her chest and stood up again, "and I'm Psycotica!" Fogstar looked at Rebecca pitifully and flashed a look at Anomily. "Yes, yes, and now that she knows our names, she can be killed? Right, Foggy?" She looked down at Fogstar expectantly, and as he shook his head, she scoffed and crossed her arms impatiently.

"What would be the point of killing her anyways? We could just give her a room and have another person stay with us!" Pupil seemed to like the idea quite a lot as he flapped up to hover over Anomily.

"We don't have another room though, and not nearly enough food." Psycotica looked around and went into what looked like a kitchen to check what their pantry looked like. "See? We need to kill more people so we can eat," she said. Pupil glared at the door to the kitchen as Psycotica walked out, holding a small jar with an inch of yellowed liquid in it.

"What about we untie her?" Fogstar added hopefully. Anomily glared down at him and stooped to his level.

"What makes you think we have time for another being, Fog-" Psycotica cut Anomily off.

"Great idea, kitty, we can at least let her stay for lunch!" And with that, Pupil and Anomily went to the kitchen, Psycotica pulled out a knife and cut the ropes around Rebecca.

"Thanks…" Rebecca said. She spotted Fogstar trying to detach from Anomily's gaze. When he did so successfully he went to stand beside Rebecca, they exchanged glances and walked to the kitchen, unsurely. Anomily was arguing with Pupil about what to eat. Psycotica was pulling out plates and lining them up on the big grey marble island they had. The room was covered in little red stains and smelled faintly of decay and medication. Anomily pulled the fridge open and took out three jars of spices; Rebecca doubted they were from plants. Pupil flew over to the stove and turned it on. Green flames erupted from the top of it and slowly grew closer to the burnt stove's top. Fogstar had begun putting silverware and napkins on the table; they were all smudged and dirty. Psycotica screamed at him to use the new ones, which he glanced at and then pulled out red-stained ones from under the table and set them around instead. Psycotica seemed fine with this as her expression of hate rinsed away. Anomily glared at Fogstar from across the kitchen again, Rebecca sat down at the end of the table, covered in a purple tablecloth laced with black spiders. Pupil seasoned the plates with a ginger-colored powder and, what looked like a smile, covered his eyeball. He picked up the dishes and flew them to the table. Rebecca realized that there were six plates and only five people. Just as she was going to ask about it, the door burst open from across the kitchen.

"I'M HOOOME!" was shouted across the room as a bloodied body was thrown on the floor right next to Rebecca.

Sprizx

Rebecca almost screamed, Fogstar gagged from across the table and turned his head away from the sight. Anomily shot him a look before Psycotica stood up and clapped her hands excitedly.

"I caught em' that'll teach them to stop stealin' our stuff!" A white cat was standing on top of the body, grey spots and stripes interrupted his fur, with blood spattered everywhere. He had an eye patch and a black tunic loosely strapped around him. He landed on the body of a particularly tan and pathetic looking man. Psycotica started clapping madly; Anomily glared at Fogstar, slowly clapping her hands. The cat dug through one of the being's pockets before pulling out five gemstones, a moonstone flew out of his hand and hung itself on his right ear. A triangular-shaped peridot made its way over to Anomily and settled on a black string hanging around her neck. A jagged zircon stuck itself to one of Pupil's wings, and two diamond-shaped gems whirled around Psycotica as she laughed with glee, there was a tourmaline and an alexandrite. The cat lifted his head and pushed the body to the end of the table in front of Fogstar.

"Who are our guests?" He asked, poking Fogstar, of which he didn't approve.

"Oh! We should introduce you! This is Sprizx!" Sprizx puffed up with pride and jumped up to his seat at the table.

"This is Foggy, you know him, I think. This one... we have no idea, really." Anomily scoffed, picking up her fork and digging into her food.

"Fogstar," He corrected, scowling at Anomily. "And I found her on the road, what is your name?" Rebecca looked at the table for a moment,

"M-My name is uh... Tess," she looked over at Fogstar, who nodded, relieved.

"Hmmm, kitty, didn't you say her name was Rachel? No, wait that was me." Psycotica picked up the bloodied napkin and wiped her face.

"I'm confused, is his name Foggy or kitty?" Sprizx looked over at an unimpressed Fogstar who was going to correct him before Anomily cut him off.

"His name is Fogstar, but *friends* call him Foggy," she said, holding up a hand dramatically, "I, of course, am a friend."

Plans

"Friend? Anomily nobody would ever be *your* friend." Sprizx rolled his eye from next to Anomily as she pushed him causing him to fling food everywhere. Fogstar was looking very uncomfortable at this point. Anomily and Sprizx were fighting now, Pupil glanced over at them every few seconds but Psycotica didn't seem to mind.

"Can I borrow...Tess, for a second?" Fogstar asked Psycotica; she nodded her head blankly as he got up and gestured Rebecca to follow.

As she got up, she realized that Psycotica's eyes had changed to blank white and that she had hunched over. She stood up straight, quite quickly, and shouted, "We got another one! STOP FIGHTING AND LISTEN TO ME IDIOTS!" as Rebecca walked out of the kitchen, closing the door behind her.

"I just want you to know I'm not working with them," Fogstar said, sitting down to look her in the eyes.

"Kinda figured."

"Good, so do you have any ideas of how to escape yet?" Rebecca lowered her head, Fogstar seemed to understand. "That's okay; I think we need to distract them with something and then run. They can't leave their swamp, so if we get out, it should be okay. I should also tell you a few things before you go." She eyed him quizzically. "First off, Sprizx is a guardian and has no real powers besides being annoying. Pupil is referred to as evil but he doesn't do anything and won't hurt you, he's too sacred for that. Anomily controls time anomalies and can reverse time, be careful of that, and she wouldn't mind killing you. Lastly, Psycotica is insanity, that's not a joke, she feeds off of violence, fear, and mental issues be very careful of her." This warning seemed slightly concerning considering Psycotica was just a child; then again, astral beings didn't age.

"Uh...okay? Are you sure Psycotica's evil? I mean, she's just a kid." Rebecca looked behind her at the door.

"Do you know when the first person was declared insane?" He asked flatly as she turned her head to look at him.

"No, when?"

"Well, whenever it was, that's when she was created, we'll leave after lunch, okay?"

Escape

"Wait, so when something happens for the first time, that's when you're created?" Fogstar was about to open the door when Rebecca decided to stop him with a question.

"Yes, not the guardians of course but beings like me that control something are created when that thing is created. It's quiet simple actually," he answered, opening the door to the sound of hysterical laughing from the other side.

"Yes, that's a wonderful idea Sprizx," Anomily said bitterly staring down at Sprizx who was laughing more than he probably should. Pupil looked quite uncomfortable flapping in his seat on the left side of the table. Psycotica was giggling from her seat and banging her hand down on the table, as Fogstar sat down she looked up, choking back sadistic laughter.

"K-Kitty should know our plans!" Anomily shot up and tried to stop the Psycotica, but the look that she threw across the table must have changed her mind as she sat down, scowling at both Psycotica and Fogstar. "Sprizx says we should start setting up traps for the intruders that come in and steal our things. He says we should kill them! I think it's a wonderful idea, don't you?" Fogstar turned quite pale, Anomily snickered at him.

"Wait- no that's wrong, you can't kill anyone. I thought you couldn't di-" Rebecca started, but Fogstar shot a look at her, she stopped as every head turned to her.

"Wrong?" Psycotica asked from beside her.

"Death is not wrong; he is a very truthful and-" Pupil cut Anomily off.

"I don't think that's what she meant. Why do you think death is wrong, Tess?" Pupil inquired from across the table.

"Death isn't wrong; *murder* is."

"Well, isn't murder just a way to speed up death?" Sprizx said from the floor. The table erupted with cheers and clapping, along with some laughter. Pupil just flapped silently and stared at the floor. "Exactly, don't you get it? We're just puttin' the poor things outta their misery," Sprizx said, causing the table to erupt in laughter again.

"That's not right; you're insane!" Rebecca shouted, and the whole table stopped immediately. Fogstar nearly face palmed before realizing maybe he shouldn't then glanced a pitying look at her before diving under the table with Pupil.

"And is that a bad thing?" Psycotica asked. Rebecca realized that she was the living embodiment of insanity and got immensely scared.

"No, it's a figure of speech where I come from," Rebecca said, braver than she had expected. Fogstar poked his head out and looked at her with a 'what are you doing? STOP!' face.

"And where exactly do you come from?" Anomily said from the other side of her. Fogstar was shaking his head violently and mouthing 'no' before getting pulled down by Pupil's wing.

"Somewhere you've never been." She was surprised at her confidence. Never in her life had she stood up for herself in this way.

"I've traveled multiple realms; I'm *sure* I have seen where ever you are from," Sprizx hissed, scowling beneath the table and jumping up to his seat next to Anomily. Fogstar fought back up to the top of the table and was clambering his way onto his chair.

"Look, I know you're a guardian, but really, you have probably never been to where I'm from." Rebecca was looking at Psycotica's angry face, her eyes had started to turn white again, and she looked as if she would jump out of her seat and strangle her at any time.

"Stop delaying what you're saying." Psycotica's voice had grown cold and hoarse; she was practically screaming but quietly. Fogstar signaled toward the door, as Psycotica got up from her chair and walked across the table. Rebecca realized what he was saying and mouthed, 'are you crazy?' He nodded and got up, flipping his tail and twitching his ear nervously. Nobody cared that he was leaving except Pupil, who must have said something from under the table because Fogstar whispered to him and then creaked the door open slowly.

"What are you doing kitty?" Psycotica's eyes changed back to their usual green and looked at Fogstar pitifully. Rebecca thought this was the perfect moment and bolted out the door as Fogstar joined her at a run. They heard screaming behind them and flapping, Pupil's voice begging Psycotica not to hurt them. Anomily was chasing them and with every second getting a bit closer as her clocks hands ticked back. They made their way through the droopy trees and squishy ground, the sun lighting their faces as they ran. Fogstar pulled out in front and reached the abrupt end of the swamp; Anomily was practically right behind Rebecca, and as she crossed the barrier, Anomily smacked into it like a brick wall.

"ARGH!" She grabbed her face and moved one of her clock hands back into place. "You will pay for this!" Rebecca didn't want to stay for the rest of her speech, she felt her Chrysalis state flare up for some reason but swallowed it down and decided to keep running. Fogstar took a second but caught up with her eventually. They were panting by the time they were out of sight.

Desire

Rebecca had been walking with Fogstar for a very long time. The path they were on was extraordinarily beautiful; the trees grew close but not nearly close enough to feel surrounded. Clouds above let through bright light cascading down upon the world below. Fogstar looked like he regretted all of his life decisions.

"What's wrong?" Rebecca asked, expecting him to get overprotective again, but he didn't. He didn't even hear her; he just kept walking, so she asked again louder, and he looked up at her and apologized.

"Sorry, just thinking."

"How did you know all of them? How did Anomily know you?" Fogstar seemed like he didn't mind answering this. Rebecca couldn't tell if he didn't care to talk to her because of what happened in Nostalgia. Or if this wasn't what he had been thinking about.

"Anomily wasn't always a bad person. When Halo chose me to be the savior's guide, Anomily was still one of the most important people in Halo's court. I don't know why she went with Psycotica, but about when Timezone was born, she decided she didn't want to be part of the family anymore."

"Wait, who's Timezone?" Rebecca was surprised at how absent Fogstar was in the conversation, which was very unlike him.

"Well, Anomily has two siblings, Clockwork and Timezone. She is the daughter of Time, after all."

"Oh, well, um… anyways, where are we going next? Another stop or…" she trailed off as Fogstar looked at her and smiled a bit.

"No, no more stops. Next city over is Hope."

"What's Hope?" And at that moment, the trees parted to reveal a giant grey tower with an overhang sporting a yellow crystal hovering in between its arches.

"What is Hope? Rebecca, did you pay any attention when we were planning where to go?" She shook her head, staring up in awe at the tower. Fogstar laughed at her, and then, clearing his throat for effect, he added, "It's where Halo lives."

Hope

As they entered Hope a feeling crossed over both of them, Fogstar looked happy again. Many beings filled Hope, all bustling through the cramped streets, smiling happily and talking about the new plans for the Astral Plane. The whole place was beautiful; tents and shops lined every street, one of them was so crowded with beings she couldn't see inside it. Hurried footsteps sounded on the paths. Fogstar looked and asked if she wanted to wait in *that* line. When she said no, he laughed and waved her on. Green leaves fell from invisible trees onto the white brick walkway as feet crushed them and made them float away. Once an off-white cat in red and orange beads winked and waved, causing a wave of wind to blow in their faces, Fogstar smiled and waved back as she danced her way through the crowds. As they walked farther and farther she realized that they were walking in a spiral, soon the market came to an end and in its place was a garden of green bushes and leaves. A few small trees planted here offered little shade from the comfortable heat hitting their faces. Butterflies and grasshoppers flew and chirped through the garden happily, and pink flowers bloomed in every place they landed. As they walked through the sunlight, another path led back into the market, Fogstar guided them back in even though they had just made it out of there. Soon they were faced with more beings; these seemed to know everyone they saw and made conversation with just about every being that walked past them. A few addressed Fogstar commenting on how he had 'another one' traveling with him. After walking for about five minutes, another being confronted them, a tall woman with draped silk around her arms pulled them aside; she had six eyes and shoulder-length golden hair. All of her clothes were in pastel pink, green, and purple. She had a soft and airy voice. "Um, excuse me. Do you know where Gemstone is?"

"Yes, right down there, take a left, and once you see the crowded shop go in there, I'm sure she will be happy to help you," Fogstar said as he took her hand and shook it with his paw.

"Ah, alright thank you. I can never seem to find my way. My name is Deepdream by the way. And you are?"

"Fogstar," He responded as Deepdream's hands sprouted eyes, "have a good day."

"Why are birthstones so important?" Rebecca asked, watching Deepdream skip away.

"Well, we get them when made and put our energy in them. The birthstones aren't a source of magic, but they keep us alive. Without them we lose power and get very tired, if we don't have one for long enough we, well… die." Fogstar cleared his voice at this part and carried on. "Gemstone is always very busy because every being needs a birthstone, even the guardians."

"Who exactly is Gemstone?"

"She is an astral being who has been around since the beginning of time. She takes the form of a human 'bunny.'" Rebecca imagined a bunny trying to heat a furnace and cutting gems in half to give out to the crowd. She laughed, and Fogstar gave her a look.

"What is your birthstone?" Fogstar pointed at his earring and replied.

"Amethyst, what is yours again?" He asked. Rebecca didn't know; no one had ever asked her that question before.

"Uh... I don't know, actually..." She said as Fogstar raised an eyebrow and asked which month she was born in, she replied with January.

"January, huh? Well, then it must be garnet."

"What is your birthday anyway?" she asked. Fogstar laughed nervously.

"I uh... didn't know until recently, so don't laugh."

"You didn't know when you were born...made?" Fogstar looked at her with an 'excuse me, but what do you take me for?' face and shook his head.

"It's February 14th... Valentine's Day-" He growled at the idea as Rebecca laughed at him, a golden tent was beside them. As Rebecca finished laughing at Fogstar, she heard a voice and saw a figure. The figure's eyes lit up at the sight of Fogstar, and she wrapped an arm around them and pulled them inside the tent.

Yearly

The interior was huge and filled with the smell of flowers and smoke. Cloths hung from the ceiling blocking off sections for the many beings inside. Voices chatted and laughed as Fogstar stumbled through the door to stand next to Rebecca.

"It's SOOOO nice to see you again, APRIL, MARCH! COME HERE FOGGY'S BACK!" A short girl shouted, holding Rebecca's hand, she let go and laughed. Her blonde hair tied up into two buns and she was wearing a white shirt tucked under a pink skirt, she had two feathery wings on her back. Two other beings popped their heads around the corners and came running. One was tall and lengthy with paint all over his clothes, paintbrushes spilling out of his pockets. He had short brown hair and loads of freckles. The other wore a cozy grey sweater with jeans patched every few inches. He had a flower crown and two feathery balls flapping madly and almost lifting him off the ground.

"Foggy!" The flower boy said, smiling and hugged him. Fogstar awkwardly cleared his throat. "Who's this girl?"

"I have no idea." The other boy said as he walked up to shake Rebecca's hand. "I'm April, by the way."

"March." The boy in the flower crown smiled and called for his mother, who came rushing in her hair pulled into brown-blonde pigtails. She looked rushed, busy, and exhausted.

"And I'm May!" The girl in front of her mother was very hyper, running around and clapping violently.

"HEY! Keep it down; I'm sure some of us are doing things." A male voice shouted from across the tent, 'mhhm's,' and 'yeah's' came from the other spaces.

"Sorry, December! Kids keep it down; May stop pulling people inside the tent. Hello, I'm sorry for my daughter." The other woman said, her voice was kind and overworked. Fogstar said hello and then tried to leave, but May stopped him and asked him to stay for tea. He sighed, looked pitifully at the door, and walked farther inside. March jumped with joy, and April escorted Rebecca to a table in the middle of the tent. A girl with big circle glasses and a black bob sat reading a book. A grey cat sat next to her, under her enormous green leaf wings, with a gem in his tail. They continued talking about the book they were reading before looking up at the others, nodding, and then leaving the table.

"Sorry, June, wanna show Foggy around?" May shouted. June smiled and shook her head. Fogstar sat down and drank his tea while listening to the other's rambling. Rebecca found the stories quite impressive, one was about how Halo had 'blessed' Hope last week cause' a new savior was here. March stared off wondering who it might be and wondering if he would ever meet them. Both Fogstar and Rebecca laughed, he blushed at them and stormed off.

"Well, well, well." A new being walked in. He was wearing what looked like a vampire costume and devil horns on top of his curly brown hair. A substantial yellow smile painted over his frowning face. Devil wings sprouted from his back as he sat down in the chair and took a bottle of wine from the top of it. "Who in the Astral Plane stole Feb's wine?" Just then, a girl stormed into the room. Her black hair was tangled and wet. She wore a tattered grey-blue dress and fishnets. But what surprised Rebecca the most was the black tears that rolled down her cheeks. She wasn't crying; they were just there; she grabbed the bottle from the boy's hand and stomped away.

"February's mad," May said, looking over at the boy in the vampire costume. "October, what did you do?"

"Hey! Don't blame me! I didn't do anything!" October glared at the table, sighed, and left. He looked a little sad, May looked at April, who nodded and went after him.

"Well, I do suppose that you do have to leave… bye, Foggy." May let them go and opened the tent door for them. The bright light blinded Rebecca as she walked out and said goodbye. Fogstar thanked them and smiled at May, suddenly covered in a dark shadow; she looked up, laughed nervously, and ran back into the tent, shouting 'MOM.' Fogstar turned around before Rebecca, and he smiled and told the man behind him that he was happy to see him. The man standing behind them had a clock for a head, it was gold-rimmed, and a chain led down to a pocket on a checkered gold and brown waistcoat. He was dressed in different shades of gold and dirty yellows. Unlike Anomily, his clock hands didn't move back; they ticked perfectly, and when they reached twelve, a faint chime came from the back of his head.

"How nice to see you again, Clockwork," Fogstar said, nudging Rebecca so she would say hello too. The clock smiled and shook Rebecca's hand lightly; he was wearing black gloves that covered a faint sound of cogs.

"Thank you, Fog-star, but I have al-rea-dy met our you-ng sav-ior." Fogstar raised an eyebrow, and Clockwork winked at Rebecca. It was at that moment that she realized something. Clockwork was the voice that talked in her Chrysalis State.

Clockwork

"Um… F-Fogstar?" Rebecca stuttered; Fogstar looked up at her quizzically. "Do you think we can… trust Clockwork?" Fogstar looked at her like she was crazy and whispered to her as Clockwork turned around and led them down the street

"Of course, it is Clockwork after all! I have known him since…" He paused and thought about it but couldn't seem to name how far back their meeting was. "Why do you ask?"

"Uh…" She looked over at Clockwork, who was leading them to the tower in the center of Hope, through more tents of people saying 'hello' to Fogstar and Clockwork. "Um… well…"

"Is this about when he met you the first time? I was wondering how that happened." Fogstar looked around and smiled at his surroundings. He looked so… happy.

"He talked to me when I was first in my Chrysalis state. I don't know how, but he was there…" Rebecca looked at Fogstar, who clearly did not believe this story. When he finally realized that she wasn't lying, he stared up at Clockwork with a very confused face.

"How in the name of Halo did you…?" Clockwork looked down at Fogstar with a curious expression.

"How in the name of Halo did I do what?" He asked. At first, Rebecca thought he was covering up the fact that he had somehow talked to her in her Chrysalis form, but after a few seconds of staring at him, she realized he genuinely had no idea about what they were talking about. Fogstar seemed to drop the question. They walked for a few extra minutes, Fogstar glancing between Clockwork and Rebecca every few seconds and trying to figure out how something like that was possible. Finally, Clockwork dropped them off outside the giant tower, which Rebecca saw was made of gray concrete. There were no windows, and the tower was so tall it could've touched the clouds if they were back on Earth, that is. He said his goodbyes and walked back towards the many things that Hope had to offer. Fogstar smiled at her and walked up to the entrance, and two guards were there. They immediately recognized Fogstar and let them pass through the grand door. She took a deep breath and prepared herself to meet Halo. As she stepped through the door, bright lights hurt her eyes, and all the voices of Hope were blocked out as the door closed behind her, which left them in complete silence.

Tower

Inside was dark, but a lantern soon lit up, a guard waved them up white marble steps into a second room. It was bright and made of gray stone walls. There were no windows, but white light flooded in all the same. Guards dressed in silver armor bowed as they walked across a yellow carpet that led to another door, this one locked. As Rebecca was about to ask where it led, a guard stepped up and unlocked the door.

"Fogstar." He said bowing; Fogstar smiled and bowed his head before leading Rebecca into another room. This one had no walls and no pillars; it was just floating with nothing there. Wide white stairs scattered around the circular room, which led down into the festival through which they had just walked. Beings ran up the stairs letting small shadows form on the steps as little lanterns glowed brightly lighting up the walls. The whole room had stalls set up selling a variety of objects from what looked like the entire Astral Plane. Beings bustled around in the one open level of Halo's tower. They were all so happy, and even Fogstar was smiling slightly. She saw one actual window interrupting one of the walls, its glass was stained white, and the beings around it seemed to avoid it. Rebecca walked over to it and looked out upon an empty wasteland of dead grass. It was horrible, and even with the happiness around her, she couldn't help feeling absolutely terrible, like this was the end of the world. Fogstar looked as scared as she was; he had his tail tucked between his legs and his ears pressed back.

"That's... were it happened." He choked on his words and had to pause a few times just to get them out. She realized what he meant and looked out at the wasteland again. A war had been fought there, blood splattered on the dying grass, tears had fallen into the blackness of despair, and Nightshade himself had been standing right there. She could see why Fogstar was so hesitant about looking out the window; he cleared his throat and led her across the room to more marble stairs. These stairs stood behind a white gate, the guard standing there looked at them and without warning almost tripped over his desk to press the button that opened the gate. Fogstar said thank you, and the man nodded, smiling awkwardly. As she walked up the stairs to the next room, she saw at least a dozen maids and butlers rushing around straightening flower pots and dusting the stair railings. Little flying grasshoppers floated around squeaking polite orders; one of the butlers caught sight of them and almost screamed. His hair tied back into a black ponytail; he nearly knocked over a maid in his rush to get to them.

"Madam! Monsieur! So sorry!" The man had a very heavy French accent; at this point, the whole room had stopped to look at them. One of the women almost screamed.

"It's fine. I wasn't expecting service." Fogstar politely tried to stop him as the butler started to apologizing profusely. They seemed like room service, people must be able to stay here. She assumed they had visitors but a whole floor devoted to staff? Seemed a bit extra. Even more stairs led through more rooms, mostly the same but one. It was about the same height as seven floors and dedicated to one thing, a garden. Green plants clung to the walls and competed with the vines for space. Flowers bloomed on the tall plants that led to the ceiling of the room. A light drizzle of misty rain fell on the floor, giving the plants little dew drops. Butterflies and other critters flew around with tiny watering cans or little hoses; they poked and prodded a few stubborn plants and stray leaves. Walking up the white spiral stairs felt like a dream, Fogstar smiled at her disappointment when they got to the top. More rooms were in the way, and by the time they got to the top, it felt like it had been hours of climbing stairs and saying thank you to guards. At the top, the walls split into twelve long hallways, Rebecca looked down at Fogstar; he caught her gaze and stared up at her.

"Why are all these hallways here? It didn't look like the tower got any thicker at the top..."

"Oh, well, uh... These are more safety measures than anything..." As Fogstar said this, a butler carrying a plate of what looked like fruit, rushed across the room and into one of the halls. "Nightshade's followers tried to break in once, it didn't go so well for them, but Halo thought we should put in some safety measures... actually, *I* thought we should put in some safety measures, and the court ruled her out..." Rebecca glanced down one of the halls.

"What's down there? Wait, *you're* part of Halo's court?" Fogstar glanced at her, slightly offended.

"Excuse me? But um... yes. I do work with Halo. As for your first question, it depends on which one. Some have traps and lava; others lead to storage rooms, which go to kitchens. One of them goes to Halo's throne room or as she calls it..." Fogstar sighed. "Never mind. Do you want to guess at which one?" Rebecca looked around; all the hallways looked the same.

"What will you do if I guess wrong?" Fogstar snickered and sat down to wait.

"Throw you in a pit of lava." He teased.

"That one?" She pointed at the one to her left; she felt like it was the one.

"Hmm, you really are the savior... come on, let's go." He led her down the hall, the way to meet Halo.

Halo

The hall was dark, but as they walked, a soft light started to form at the end of the tunnel. As they neared it, the light grew brighter, and she realized what was at the end. Another garden shined with yellowed light, cascading down from a glass ceiling that led to nowhere. Green vines hung, growing fruits and plants floated in their pots while being tended to by yellow butterflies, it was wonderful. She could just make out lavender growing with marigolds in a plant holder from behind a rather large white arch. The bugs seemed to realize someone was here and quickly flapped their way over to the wall; Fogstar looked kind of scared as the butterflies started picking flowers off their branches. It took a minute, but when they finished, they placed two flower crowns on each of their heads. Rebecca's had three morning-glories and a few pink flowers nestled in it. White puff balls floated on the leaves of her crown also drizzled with lavender leaves. She looked down at Fogstar, who looked a little embarrassed wearing his crown of yellow dandelions and lavender stocks. He shook it off. Rebecca laughed and watched him open a hatch in the floor. It was dark inside, but she stepped in anyway, it turned out to be a hole. As she fell, Rebecca felt like screaming, but her descent seemed to be slowing down. She noticed little yellow lights struggling to keep her afloat.

"You were supposed to walk," Fogstar said calmly, treading on the lights. They came upon a lighted hallway, and as Rebecca walked into it, she realized that there was something there, a throne.

As the light cascaded in from the many windows, Rebecca realized there was someone else in here; it was another cat. Her fur was bright white, and her feather wings shuffled around to fit in her chair. A glowing yellow halo looped around her ears. Rebecca realized that this was the queen of the Astral Plane. She was talking to someone, though; a lean looking girl in a long, lacey, black gown was whispering hoarsely to her. Halo nodded and said something back as the girl tucked her messy black hair behind her ear, revealing a tired face and a beetle shaped crown on her head. The girl seemed to notice them and bowed to Halo, running away in panic.

"Oh! ...Mune!" Halo sighed and looked at the door through which Mune had run. "What is it now, S- Oh." She turned around and glanced at Fogstar before realizing he was back; then she noticed Rebecca and grinned. She looked back down at Fogstar, who bowed down. Rebecca figured she should too, and right before she did, Halo called out to them from her throne. "No, no need for that! Come here, let me see you, oh." Halo was practically jumping up and down in excitement. Feathers were scattered everywhere from the flapping of her immense wings as she fell out of her throne to rush over to Rebecca.

"Your Majesty, the Savior." Fogstar gestured to Rebecca; she wasn't expecting Halo to be this... normal. She thought she would be super formal and have incredibly high expectations, apparently not though.

"Oh, how was your trip, dear? I hope it wasn't too long... How many Nightshade Followers did you have to- Oh Fogstar, how many attacked her?" She looked a bit worried at asking this question. As Fogstar was about to answer, she cut him off. "Oh, never mind, I don't want to know... Well, then let us eat! You must be starving." Now that

Rebecca thought about it, she hadn't eaten in a while... Fogstar hadn't either; he must be famished too.

"You have a really nice queen," Rebecca whispered to Fogstar as they followed her through another grand hallway of marble. Fogstar smiled and said, 'yes' absentmindedly. As they neared the end, another great room came into view, chefs and butlers were rushing around trying to straighten a huge yellow tablecloth on a white table. They all took seats, Fogstar sat down next to Rebecca and Halo across from her. Halo smiled as a waiter pulled out a pen and paper and looked at Halo with a tired yet still respectful gaze.

"The usual for us please, what about you, Savior?" Rebecca looked around for a second, wondering if she was serious.

"Uh... is there a menu?" She asked, confused. Fogstar snickered in his chair next to her.

"You can have *anything* you want in my kitchens." Halo smiled from across her and shot a look at Fogstar.

"Uh...so like...pizza?" Neither of them seemed to know what that was, she sighed and explained. "It's like circle bread with tomato sauce on it and then cheese and pepperoni, and then you bake it." The waiter standing next to Halo nodded and jotted something down on his pad.

"I agree with Halo, the usual." Fogstar added as the waiter wrote it down; he seemed a lot more comfortable with this order than pizza.

"Ugh, Foggy, I don't understand how you can eat that, *all* the time," Fogstar replied to Halo's comment, but Rebecca wasn't listening. She just wanted her food to get here. Six men rushed out of two big double doors and set down a few plates, Fogstar had two, Halo had three, and Rebecca had only one. As she waited for the waiter to pull off her lid, she hoped she didn't have to eat burnt cheesy bread.

Complications

What lay before her was probably the best pizza she had ever had. Halo was scolding Fogstar on his bland taste and trying to force him to eat something else, which he refused.

"Halo, let me *eat.*" Fogstar was getting fed up being told he was boring. Halo sighed and told him it would be better if he tried new things. Rebecca didn't expect Halo to be this way; she was a lot cooler than she had thought she would be. But at the same time, it didn't seem like she took anything that seriously. Then again, she could be acting like that because she didn't get to do it often. First impressions were very important. The door opened again and Clockwork came in. He sat down one seat away on Rebecca's right and smiled at Halo.

"My Queen... there has been a bit of a... prob-lem." Clockwork looked quite uncomfortable and kept looking over pleadingly at Rebecca and Fogstar.

"What... problem Clockwork?" Halo blinked a few times and then seemed to realize what he meant and cleared her throat. "*That* problem...please excuse me, Savior, Fogstar." She got out of her chair and accompanied the sweating Clockwork out the door.

"Fogstar, what was that about?" He looked over at her and shrugged though she could tell he had an idea. "Fogstar don't lie to me." He sighed and shifted in his seat.

"I don't know, but I'm guessing it has something to do with Nightshade." Fogstar seemed to feel the same as he looked slightly alarmed like she was. A few minutes later, Halo came back and sat back down to eat the rest of her food. They remained silent for the whole time, although Halo desperately tried to create a conversation. Clockwork had left for the most part and only poked his head in a few times to make sure they were still there. Rebecca hated the silence and decided to ask a question.

"What does Clockwork do? Is he in your court to?" Halo looked endlessly thankful for the start of a conversation.

"Well yes, he is part of the court, but he is also an advisor. They are the beings who have... better ideas and morals than some other beings." Halo looked a bit awkward using 'better' to describe her advisors.

"Is Fogstar an advisor?" Rebecca asked, but that question was more or less discarded because of Clockwork, running in, panting.

Endless

Clockwork ran over to Halo and whispered in her ear. She sighed, clearly irritated, and excused herself, muttering to Clockwork as she walked out the room. She turned around and gestured Fogstar to come with her, he froze and looked over at Rebecca.

"Go." She mouthed at Fogstar who gave her a pleading look and then hesitantly got up and left with Halo and Clockwork. Leaving Rebecca all alone in a castle about which she knew nothing. At some point a few minutes later, she decided she didn't want to stay here, so she got up and pushed open the big marble doors into the new, yellow-lit, narrow hallway leading in a thousand different directions. She wandered through the halls, spiraling around the turns and finally heard voices coming from around the corner, she stopped to listen.

"I know Graphic found him, and now he is getting in the way with his obliviousness to the situation." Halo's tone said she was annoyed with the "situation." Clockwork stammered next to her.

"W-Well your Maj-es-ty, that's not why I- ne-ver mind… Leaf, he foun-d a be-ing named Sta-tic so they have a-no-ther mem-ber on top of that and," Fogstar cut him off.

"What are we going to be doing with the Savior? We can't just leave her there!" Fogstar sounded mad, but the silence that followed made it seem like Clockwork was offended.

"I appreciate that Fogstar but as a group we need to talk about this, if you want to leave to go get her, you can, but

I need to talk to Clockwork and you right now." Fogstar didn't respond to this.

"Your Ma-jes-ty I- well, I think it would be best if we sent some-one there? I mean, Mune could... I don't know... or some-one else in the- the coun-cil." Clockwork sounded out of breath, his stuttering wasn't helping the air of worry wafting from around the corner.

"I know, I think it's a good idea, Clockwork, but I don't know if anyone is free right now..." Fogstar cut off Halo again.

"Your Majesty, I would love to go but she shouldn't listen to this, and besides my room may or may not be *taken* by Strand." Fogstar spat this last part like it was Nightshade. Halo finished at this point.

"Fogstar I know you and the Savior are friends, and I promise you this conversation isn't the most important thing, your room is still taken, I know, so go to the guest room. I didn't want the *Savoir* to stay in a greyscale room of foggy torture, and I assure you Strand is *not* enjoying it." Everything was silent, even Clockwork's rapid breathing stopped. Halo sighed and seemed to walk away with Clockwork as the sound of ticking faded slowly.

"Oh, I will get you back for this..." Fogstar muttered, along with other, inaudible things as he walked around a yellowed pillar and bumped right into Rebecca. He looked up at her, and his ears lay back, "How much of that did you hear?" he asked. Rebecca laughed.

"Not much, seems like you guys are dealing with something right now?" Fogstar gave her a look.

"Ever since this thing came up she's been so busy, and I don't know, I guess I just don't like things like Nightshade or your protection being ignored..." Rebecca pitied him; he was lonely with no one to turn to since Abbigail. She wasn't exactly glad to take up the responsibility of being a place for venting but as long as he was still useful she could put up with it. She smiled sadly at him, and he did the same before realizing that they were standing somewhere they probably weren't supposed to be.

"Uh... We shouldn't be here; we need to find our room... Where did Halo say it was again? Guest room? Yes... right." Fogstar went into a kind of trance as he tried to remember where this 'guest room' was in the massive tower. They kept turning twisty corners and walking up and down small flights of stairs. The lighting kept changing from yellow to white. The sun beat down from an unknown source and lightly grazed their faces as they walked around. They finally reached a massive white marble door and stepped inside; the walls were made of slate and painted a bright white. A large bed sat to the side of the room covered in white bedding and yellow pillows. There was a grey dresser with drawers that kept shaking and a window ledge with yellow curtains swaying in the light breeze that came from the non-existing outside; in fact, the window ledges' view was just a white void. Fogstar sat down on a yellow pillow and grabbed a scroll out of one of his fog clouds. Rebecca sat down on the bed and looked out the window.

"What is there to do here exactly?" She asked. In truth, she was quite bored, without even looking up Fogstar pointed at the dresser and went back to making a pen float across the paper, which was also floating in the air. She got up and walked over to the chest of drawers and sat down in the yellow chair in front of it. She looked in the mirror at her messy self and wanted to brush her hair. Although it might be more fun to see what her family was doing about the situation right now, she pulled open a drawer expecting to see a hairbrush. Instead, she found a glistening silver mirror, as she held it up Fogstar finally looked away from his scroll and looked at her in what seemed to be amazement.

She looked into the mirror, and Fogstar floated up to get a closer look.

Mirror

"Oh, I remember this." He smiled slightly at it and then realized that Rebecca had no idea what it was. "This dresser gives you whatever you need or want, that mirror can show you anything or anyone in any realm. We tried to find my parents with it once, but it didn't work..." Rebecca gave him a pitiful look and asked how it worked. "Well, you just say who you want to see, it can only find one person, of course, but I guess it only works when you know who you're looking for."

"Um... do I have to say their name or..." He shrugged and floated up to her shoulder to look around it. "Uh... Rachel Miller..." The face of the mirror swirled around, and the glass then showed a picture of her mom, she looked tired and overworked. Her eyes were puffy, and her cheeks stained with tears as she was talking to officers. Fogstar reached a paw over her shoulder and pressed a swirl on the mirror, and the sound turned on.

"Mrs. Miller, we know your daughter is missing, but we searched the whole area, and we haven't found a trace of her." Her mother's face was lit up by the weak sunlight and red and blue flashing lights from the three police cars parked outside her house.

"I don't care if we have to search somewhere else we can. I need to find my daughter." The officer nodded and walked back to her car, her mother sniffed and hugged her brother, who had just come out. He looked worried but not like he cared much, he never cared.

"They're looking for me." She whispered, she could feel the tears welling up in her eyes as she watched her mother's desperate attempts to get her back.
"Um… so that's you're… M-Mother? And you're…?" Fogstar looked very confused.

"Yeah…my mother and my brother, Jason." Fogstar nodded, clearly still confused. She could see the TV playing inside the house. Rebecca saw a reporter saying how odd it was that there had been no fog for a few weeks. Both of them laughed together at the funny thought that mortals didn't understand; the fog being was escorting a human across a magical plane to fight an evil being of darkness. Then again, who in their right mind would guess that?

Parenting Skills

When Halo returned she looked kind of tired and told them to go to bed, Fogstar was hesitant and kept asking Halo if she was *sure* there were no problems. She kept telling him to stay and whispering to Clockwork behind the door about something called the 'Edgellion.' Who would name their… thing *that*? After a few minutes, Halo finally left, and they sat there in the slowly fading light of the white void, which was now turning yellow. Fogstar lay down with a huff on the bed and looked out the window longingly. Rebecca sat down next to him and looked at the mirror, which she had kept out just in case she wanted to see her mom again.

"Do all beings have parents?" Rebecca turned the mirror over to look at the back. Fogstar snapped out of his trance and looked at her.

"No, but some do, it's kind of complicated. Most guardians don't, but when they retire, some of them fall in love." He cleared his throat awkwardly and continued. "Some of the other beings do too and sometimes ask Halo to create new beings for them."

"How do you know that you even have parents?" Rebecca didn't mean to sound mean, but Fogstar looked a bit offended.

"Halo told me, she knows because they asked her but… I don't know it's odd. I think she knows, but… it's like she doesn't want me to know." Rebecca turned around to look at Fogstar, who was now looking at his paws sorrowfully. She felt bad for him, but there was nothing she could do about it. At least he didn't have to put up with parents, watching you, controlling everything you do. She envied the freedom he had. But now she had it too, being the Savoir and all. No school, no college, no bed times... actually as that thought sprang into her head she realized how late it actually was.

"How long are we going to stay up?" Rebecca asked, looking out into the void, which was now a dark grey, signaling nightfall. Fogstar shrugged and did the same. An hour or so of talking followed about life at home and how different the Physical realm was from the Astral Plane. Fogstar finally decided it was time to go to sleep and floated off the bed to let her pull up the sheets and tuck them around her.

"Where are you going to sleep?" Fogstar shrugged and floated up to the window sill. He sat there for a while but eventually clambered back to the bed, curling up in a ball next to her. She could hear him softly snoring and the sound of footsteps outside the door, for the first time in a while, she couldn't sleep. She saw Halo check on them at one point and smile in the doorway, but after that, there was no one. Then finally, she fell asleep.

Anticipation

When she finally woke up, Fogstar was already up and waiting for her. He led her back through the halls to the kitchens and had breakfast with the rest of the council members. Halo sat at the end of the table, she looked like she had stayed up all night. A few other members sat at the table, including the girl that was talking to Halo; her name was Mune. Clockwork was there, but he seemed distant and kept fiddling with the small golden rings strung around his neck. Another girl with red crosses all over her white nurse uniform sat eating what looked like a salad. A clock on the wall kept ticking too fast, and Halo kept telling Clockwork to calm down. Fogstar was pretty much done with everyone and pulled Rebecca outside after she finished her breakfast. They went out and, after a while, ran into May and April again. But besides that, there were no familiar faces in crowds. Today the gardens were crowded, and they could barely push through the crowds to get to the other side of Hope. Fogstar seemed stressed and worried every time he turned a corner or walked across a street. She wanted to ask why, but he didn't seem to want to answer any of her questions.

"Fogstar, is that Leaf?" Rebecca looked to her right and saw the plant-headed man walk past her; he waved and got elbowed by a much shorter girl in a red cloak with a spiky ponytail. A girl with a TV head snickered from behind them. Fogstar shrugged and looked at the ground, away from Rebecca. "Okay, why are you acting like this? I thought we were friends," she asked, he hesitated.

"I- We are, I just... I don't want to lose another friend and... and we're so close to when..." he sighed. She could tell he didn't want to talk about it.

"Oh... well, that makes sense. I thought you hated me or something." Fogstar laughed from beside her and took a deep breath.

"I guess I should just hope that... that never happens." Fogstar seemed quieter for the rest of the time that they spent walking around the market and talking to the few beings that paid any attention to them. Blooming flowers paved the path back to the tower, and as the guards opened the doors awkwardly, the lights cascaded down on them again. They stepped up the stairs, and after an hour made it to the top again, Fogstar had received another flower crown too. He went back to the guest room after dropping her off in the throne room with Halo.

"Oh, I know that being well, and I can tell something's wrong. What happened?" Halo asked, turning away from what seemed like picking a new light fixture for her throne room. The one hanging over her had appeared to have gone out. "Just use the same kind from last time." She shouted across the vast room, coming over to sit in front of Rebecca.

"Well, he doesn't want me to get killed, I guess." Halo looked up at her, obviously confused. "I don't know if I should tell you this, so I won't, but you know... I don't think he wants Abbigail to happen all over again, you know?" Halo nodded her head and grabbed a floating cup of tea laced with gold swirls.

"I don't think the Astral Plane could handle that again, really," Halo said. Rebecca felt sick listening to how much she didn't understand about how badly Fogstar felt. She knew beings didn't see Fogstar that way, but wow. Nobody even thought he had *feelings*.

"Well... anyways. I think I should get lunch... I'm starving." Halo led Rebecca back down to the long table and sat her down.

"What do you want, dear?" The waiters took her order for an ice-cream sundae and quickly brought one out for her to eat. It wasn't as good as the ones in the diner, but she didn't tell them how to make ice-cream either. She snuck a fruit that she had seen Fogstar eat once into her pocket.

Rebecca decided to try and find her room while wandering through the halls again. Once she found it, Fogstar was still there, he was sitting on the window sill and staring out into the void again.

"Hey," She said. Fogstar jumped and fell off the window in a pile on the floor. She laughed as he tried to recover and got up awkwardly. He walked over to the bed and hopped up next to her. Rebecca pulled out the fruit she had hid and gave it to Fogstar; he looked thankful, considering he hadn't eaten yet. "Halo is kind of oblivious to, like, *all* your feelings." He smiled and took a bite of the juicy purple fruit.

"Yeah... no one thinks I care about anyone..." He trailed off at this part.

"Not even Mistral?" He shook his head and looked back at the window before laying his ears back, and standing up very slowly said, "What?" When Rebecca turned her head, she saw what he had meant. The whole void had been turned black and glossy. A Nightshade follower seeped inside their room. It let out a shrill scream and thrust its melting body at them. Rebecca quickly transformed and slashed it in half before kicking it back out the window. Halo ran through the door in a panic and was screaming orders at guards. The only one she understood clearly was, "turn on the barrier" as beings shouted across the halls in fear and desperation.

"Nightshade... he's attacking!" Halo panted at them before pulling them through the door and rushing them down one of the halls.

Barrier

As Halo dragged them along, Rebecca could see the attack on the whole of Hope by Nightshade's followers. Everything had turned black and droopy, completely ruining the garden. Fogstar was running to keep up with Halo, who was now spreading her wings to gain more height and speed. Rebecca dragged her sword on the floor, leaving a horrible scratch on its surface. Fogstar fell behind, and she couldn't see him through the crowd anymore. She tried to break free of Halo, but she had a real death grip. Another Nightshade follower jumped out in front of them and screeched at Halo. She hit it in the face with one of her wings and it stumbled backward. Startled, it got up and turned its attention to Rebecca. She grabbed her sword and cut its arm off. It let out a horrible gurgle of black and then seethed back into the shadows. Fogstar wove his way back through the Nightshade followers and scrambling butlers brushing dust off his shoulder and letting out a disapproving huff at the lack of planning Halo had taken for an event like this.

"Halo, is the barrier up?" Fogstar asked, licking scattered blood off one of his paws. He looked out a window with Rebecca just in time to see a vast yellow sphere form over the whole city. Nightshade followers on the outside of the city clambered over one another in the distance. Fogstar nodded at Halo as she sighed, clearly overwhelmed.

"This is going to be a mess." Halo looked over to Rebecca, hopefully. "Savior? Can you lend your sword to destroying these monsters?" She asked over her shoulder, knocking down another Nightshade follower with her wing and stamping the puddle it left behind into the ground.

"Fogstar, would you be so kind as to escort Clockwork to th-" Fogstar cut her off.

"Sorry, my queen, NO." He flicked his tail as if offended, and before Halo could reason with him, he stalked away, calling Rebecca with him. She shrugged empathically back at Halo and followed Fogstar out of the tower. They ran off a porch at the bottom of the tower and straight into the crowd of screaming beings throwing whatever they could while trying to kick off Nightshade followers. Rebecca clutched her sword and ran towards to the nearest Nightshade follower. Fogstar tapped her on the shoulder as she slashed the last of the follower to bits and stamped him out.

"We're going to have to split up. Promise me you will be okay, the last time I left a Savior's side…" He trailed off; she could see the worried tears building up behind his brave façade. 'I promise' is the last thing she told him before he left.

Dripping

Black swirled around her as the Nightshade followers swarmed her. The heat of their goop splashed her face and ran down her neck, covering her in splatters. As she raised her sword and swiped down another Nightshade follower, it let out a scream, a horrible, hoarse screech that echoed through Hope. She could hear the angry, offended growls of the other followers as they swarmed her again. The only real thing she could do was swing at the blackness surrounding her, and for a second, she lost hope. An enormous wing came crashing into her vision, throwing followers down the paved streets. Halo came into view knocking a few more over and smiling at Rebecca.

"Are you okay?" She asked, she looked to her heels and then around where she was standing. "Where's Fogstar?"

"He went off; he said it would be easier if we didn't *try* to stick together..." Halo's expression was startled and confused, but she just muttered 'okay' and swatted more Nightshade followers to the ground, stomping them on the floor.

"Well, keep safe and try not to get swarmed again..." She waved a paw at Rebecca before flapping her wings and soaring above the many followers trying to grab her. Tackled from behind, Rebecca thrust the follower off her back, slicing it in half with her sword. She turned around to see Halo kicking the air with her leg and pointing at the Nightshade follower. Rebecca turned around and stomped on the follower; it didn't come back. She continued to use this method, taking out at least twenty followers in the time it took to get pressed up against the walls of Halo's tower. As she thrust her sword out, cutting Nightshade followers away from her, she heard a rumble in the distance, and as Rebecca looked up, she saw black start to cover the yellow barrier surrounding Hope. The followers around her let go, they hissed and spat at each other and then ran off to the source of the commotion. Then, the barrier broke. The black fell into the streets, and the followers around hissed in joy, applauding, throwing their dripping hands up at the sky. Rebecca looked up at the terrifying sight that stood in the center of her vision; held up by melting black vines, a horrible dripping black ball of a creature laughed, it was nowhere close to human.

"Thank you, my children..." His voice growled into the sky as it turned an unnatural color of grey, "I must say, Savior, I'm impressed... Battlefield Halo, you have fifteen minutes."

It was Nightshade.

Council

Halo pushed her way through the crowd from behind Rebecca. She stopped dead at the sight of Nightshade and looked up at him. He dove to the ground; the parting group of beings then let him walk across to the other side of Halo's tower. Halo's shock rinsed off the rest of the confidence the few beings left might have had. She saw Fogstar shove his way through the Nightshade followers and beings, not bothering to even say sorry. The face of relief he had when he saw Rebecca was priceless. Right before he realized she had to fight Nightshade. The thought almost made him break down into tears right then and there.

"R-Rebecca, you don't have to do this, t-they can handle themselves-" Fogstar came rushing over to her and pleaded for her not to try and fight Nightshade. Halo glanced over at him oddly, like she didn't understand he had feelings. She went over and shut Fogstar up before he could convince Rebecca not to do this.

"Savior, may I talk to you in..." Halo looked around at the many beings waiting for instruction. "...private?" She turned around and pulled Rebecca by the arm into the tower. "I HAVE FIFTEEN MINUTES TO PREPARE A WHOLE ARMY?"

Halo screamed as she paced around the room. Fogstar came rushing in behind them. "Fogstar, thank you. We could use your help in this. How do you suppose we prepare an entire army to fight Nightshade?" Her sarcasm wasn't helping.

"We can't do this." He cut her off. There were tears in his eyes, his fur scratched and bloodied all over, he looked a mess. Halo looked deathly surprised. "Rebecca please don't go out there. Y-you might not..." He broke down right in front of her for the second time. She couldn't exactly just do that though, she was being counted on to... well at least fight alongside them. Her expression must have conveyed this. Halo stood watching Fogstar for a few seconds before coming over and giving him a hug, Rebecca didn't like how weak he actually was. He seemed so different when she had met him. Fogstar looked at her like she had just betrayed the entire Astral Plane he sniffled up his tears and passed her out of the room. Rebecca smiled at Halo as she left bracing herself for the questions that never came. She was thankful Halo had some personal respect. They hurried down a corridor to a set of double doors, a sign at the top read.

'Council Room'

In big grey lettering, Halo pushed the double doors open met with the worried faces of six very different beings.

"Halo, my queen..." A woman in a nurse outfit got up and bowed, the others followed in suit. "NIGHTSHADE?" She screamed, and a whole uproar of comments erupted from the beings around the circular council room.

"Everyone please calm down. I was going to come to you earlier with the Savoir but I was busy dealing with other matters. As Clockwork must have already told you we have the Savoir here with us. Right on time! And she's going to fight with us." Halo turned her head to look at Rebecca, she nodded.

"Savior?" A big golden butterfly spoke as all the heads turned to Rebecca. "Oh, yes, *Savior*."

"Hold on, where is Fogstar?" A man with what looked like a black hole for a head stood up and spoke.

"He is uh..." Halo turned her head to a corner of the room where Fogstar was sitting down and sulking. "Not joining us for this meeting. That doesn't mean you can leave." She added, turning her head to Clockwork, who was getting out of his chair.

"Then what are we going to do?" Another girl in a very poufy pink dress laced with hearts asked. Halo thought for a moment then started talking again.

"Clockwork, how long has it been since Nightshade's ultimatum?" Everyone around the room breathed a sigh of relief.

"Ten minutes, my Queen."

"Mindscape send for Warriora and Communicate." The man with a black hole head nodded, and two purple sparks flickered in his head. "We are going to give him what he wants... an army." She brushed her wings off, and Rebecca could see Fogstar go white through his fur from across the room.

"But my queen." Another man in a white suit added from their left. "I don't want to play Fogstar, but-"

"Hey..." Fogstar sounded offended.

"There you are, we were wondering where our worried brain was... wait... Fogstar have you been cry-" Halo cut the man off as Fogstar softly sat down in his chair. He looked kind of numb. Rebecca was sure he was worried about her; it would've made her happy if she didn't think he was going to try to get her to not go. She had to go, he knew that, so why was he trying to get her to stay?

"Alright, let's do this." Halo took a deep breath as everyone in the room turned to look at her. "Today... Today we defeat Nightshade." The council room erupted with offending remarks, but both Rebecca and Fogstar stayed silent. Rebecca transformed and pulled out her sword, Fogstar stared at her in fear; she knew he'd get in the way of all the things she was now supposed to do. He silently agreed to that statement as he sniffled and took a deep breath.

Promise

Halo had pushed the double doors open and left the room talking to a woman with very knotted black hair wearing what looked like a barbarian outfit. Another man came rushing in with stacks of paper while profusely apologizing for being late. She conversed with them for a second while Fogstar made his way over to Rebecca.

"If... If something goes wrong..." He was on the verge of another breakdown, and she didn't think he would like it very much if the other council members saw.

"Nothing will go wrong; I can take care of myself." She put her hand on his shoulder, and that seemed to calm him down a bit, he smiled weakly at her and then gulped nervously. She wished he had more faith in her. Halo rushed into the room and asked for whatever the 'Edgellion' was and for someone called Graphic. Everyone was busy running around trying to find beings and calm other ones down and recruit them to join the army and plenty of other things that seemed entirely out of reach. The realization that this might be over today gave some beings hope, and they signed their names very quickly. Others remembered what happened last time and *ran* away from the clipboards. Fogstar would have been one of those people except that he had to fight because he worked for Halo. After what had seemed like five minutes passed, something happened.

"Halo, I swear, I understand you have commitment issues, but come on." Nightshade popped out of nowhere, sending a hundred beings running. "I want to fight the new Savior, and I told you, fifteen minutes. *IS THAT NOT ENOUGH*?" He whined this last part like a child that didn't want to go to bed. Halo stepped in front of everyone protectively.

"Nightshade, no, I can't prepare an army in fifteen minutes." She sounded like she had done this a million times.

"You don't need an army; I just want the Savior..." He replied. "I don't even care about the army part; I just thought you'd want one..." Halo shooed him off and kept talking to other beings about armies. Rebecca knew she would have to fight soon, that thought scared her. She was finally getting the urge to run. Could she do that? She thought she had been so brave maybe it was just the direness of this situation that made her... a coward. That's what it was, she was being a coward. Like Fogstar and all the other beings not willing to fight. Well she wasn't going to run, not until she had proven she wasn't just as worthless as the others. Halo sighed and turned to a screen to tell everyone that they were going to fight Nightshade, 'So if you're coming, let's go.' Rebecca and Fogstar followed her through the door.

Despair

A massive crowd of beings stood outside the door, waiting for Halo. When she opened the double doors to the outside the whole place erupted, she tried to calm them, but nothing would sway them or their doubt about being able to defeat Nightshade. She could hear 'But remember what happened last time!' Amongst the other things said, and she knew Fogstar heard it too because he lowered his head.

"Hey, it'll be fine, right?" Rebecca asked him, he looked up at her and nodded slightly. She could hear him sniffle, but he looked back up, put on a brave face, and stepped over to Halo.

"Alright, shut up." The crowd stopped talking immediately and looked at him. "Nightshade is here. Oh, no." His sarcasm didn't rest well with the beings. "If we all get turned into whatever we get turned into when he does whatever he does to us, then well... we tried. I'm not giving a hope speech, and frankly, I never will, so just, I don't know... follow Halo as you should." He turned and sat down behind Halo, right next to Rebecca.

"I think my job was to tell you that in a more... *hopeful* way, but Fogstar said it for me. We have to fight him, or we will all fall so... let's fight. We won once what's stopping us from doing that again?" Halo's words seemed to shut most beings up, but a few muttered things that Rebecca couldn't hear. "Nightshade can't *kill* us; as long as we defeat him things should go back to normal. But we have to fight, for all the ones before us who won't get the pleasure of being brought back in a few hours. Fight with us, or stay, but you won't be remembered as a hero then." She turned and walked around the tower. Fogstar got up and followed her, as well as the council. Rebecca caught up to Fogstar. Then turning around, she saw almost all of the beings in the crowd following Halo around the tower to the opposite side. She breathed a sigh of relief with the knowledge she wasn't fighting alone. Crossing the desolate border of Hope to Despair seemed to bring the exact effect of the name to most of the beings. She could see Fogstar regretting his choices almost immediately.

"FINALLY." Nightshade sighed from Halo's left. "Gosh, it took you so long I thought you weren't coming for a minute... kinda hurt."

Rebecca looked to her left just in time to see a whole army of black splashing Nightshade followers as well as Nightshade himself. It was by far a more terrifying thing than she had ever seen. Her sword popped into her hands again, and she braced herself for the attack.

"Aww, look at you, Savoir, just like the last one." He cooed at the crowd. "Okay, I'm bored, get em'."

Martini

Nightshade's followers took a second to process this command; many of them glanced up at him and murmured to each other. The delay was apparently very annoying to Nightshade because he started screaming a horribly hoarse screech at them. It hurt Rebecca's ears, but there was no time to waste as the Nightshade followers swarmed the battlefield knocking over the unprepared beings. As they swarmed her, she swung her sword over her head; it hit one of the followers in the face. She stomped on it until it couldn't come back and then turned her attention to the other followers. A rather large one pounced on her from behind. Through the haze of black, she tried to knock it off, it fell off her back, and she stabbed it then stomped it in with her heel. After destroying two more Nightshade followers, she got the hang of the rhythm. The ground was wet with black goo; it stuck to the bottom of her tennis shoes, staining them. She couldn't see Fogstar or Halo through the crowd; she did see a little girl dressed in black get stamped into the ground by a Nightshade follower. It said something, but she couldn't make out what exactly. Then she saw the girl jump back out with black mist swirling around her. It looked like something out of a nightmare, she thought. Then the whole world went black, and Nightshade's screeching filled her head. For a second, she felt something had happened, but when she looked up everyone... *everything* around her had the same reaction. The little girl floated down to the earth and scowled at her arm. She got trampled by another Nightshade follower. Rebecca turned around to see a sea of followers recovering from whatever the little girl had done. Rebecca slashed most of them down and turned her attention to Nightshade himself. Her confidence washed off almost as quickly as it has come. He was sipping what looked like a cocktail and laughing every time a being got trampled. She was disgusted by his behavior but realized that it wasn't the real Nightshade; it was a corrupted version of a being that used to be loved. She took a breath and walked up to him; Halo got there before her.

"Nightshade, stop this right now." Halo's voice was smooth and calming. Nightshade looked like he considered it, but it might have just been him faking.

"Wanna martini?" He asked, holding out another glass. An olive materialized on a toothpick and fell to the side with a 'clink.'

"No, Nightshade. Please stop, this isn't the answer to your problems, we can help fix you! Something!" She pleaded. Nightshade's face dropped; he turned away, still floating in the air. He looked at his martini and sighed.

"I don't need help, Halo..." He trailed off, looking away from her, he caught Rebecca's stare, and a smile broke onto his face. "OH LOOK IT'S OUR SAVIOR!" He yelled, attracting the attention of a few followers who got trampled. "Well, it is so nice to meet you. You wonderful bane of mine!" He flew down and tried to shake her hand. Rebecca pulled it away from him; he seemed slightly hurt. "What might your name be? How did you get here? Oh, I have always wanted to know." 'Don't tell him' Halo mouthed silently from behind. Nightshade floated patiently in front of her for what seemed like forever then drifted over to look at Halo.

"Is there something wrong with this one? She won't talk." Halo sighed and batted down a Nightshade follower with her wing. Rebecca stepped back and swung her sword at him. He dodged it and looked at her confusedly. He looked at Halo, and then again at her, he sighed sadly and floated up higher. Nightshade followers immediately swarmed them. Halo tried to knock them down, but they were too much for her. She fell over, and the sound of her screaming must've startled Nightshade because he dropped his martini on the ground. From 15 feet in the air, the sound of the shattering glass hurt Rebecca's ears. Nightshade turned around with black tears against the orange of his eyes.

"NO, NO, NOT HER!" He screamed, floating down to push his followers off Halo. His breathing was shaky as he helped her up; Rebecca swore his eyes turned the color of crystal. Halo shook her head and steadied herself. Nightshade turned to his followers and smashed them all to the ground with one thick, black, dripping vine slashing the life out of them all. He let go of Halo and turned to Rebecca, "You go. Do whatever you're supposed to be doing." She stood her ground.

"I'm supposed to be getting rid of you," Rebecca said, she planted her foot in the dirt as Nightshade turned his head back to her.

"On who's orders?" He asked, floating over till she could smell his ashy breath.

"Halo's," She said, Nightshade raised an eyebrow before realizing that she wasn't lying. He turned back around to look at her.

"Why?" Before Nightshade could do anything, she swung her sword at him again, he dodged it and looked offended at her again. "Fine." He said, the same black vines shooting out of the ground beside him. "You want to fight. We fight." He threw one at her that she sliced and attracted the attention of almost the whole battlefield. She could've sworn she saw Fogstar out of the corner of her eye, looking more terrified than ever. But it might've just been the light; she dodged another vine and swerved to the right. She didn't see Fogstar's outline again.

Vigorous

She tried to dodge his next attack, but it caught her shoulder, leaving a thin line of blood trickling down her shirt. It stung. She had to crouch to avoid the next vine as it swung over her head. She tried to run up to him, but he moved out of the way and threw more attacks at her. Rebecca could hear Halo trying to tell him to stop, but she was too focused on getting out of the way to make out exactly what she was saying. As one of the vines crashed down next to her, another hung over her head. It began to clamber down, but before it hit her, a cloud of fog sheltered her head. Nightshade looked at it for a split second and then looked around, trying to spot from where it came. Fogstar stepped out of the crowd, seething.

"Uh… Foggy?" Nightshade started before getting shoved to the ground by fog. He choked on it for a second but got up, clutching his throat. "Wow, uh… you seem pretty mad." He hacked out a black furball, it was disgusting. Fogstar helped Rebecca up and snapped his head back at

Nightshade. "So you're working with her? I mean that's fine, let me offer you a trade, ok? Switch sides, or kill her, I don't know. Either way I'll let you be part of my court. Like Seducia but more uh… powerful and easier to work with, most definitely."

"Never." Fogstar pulled up more fog than Rebecca had ever seen him make in his existence. Halo seemed to think so too because she stepped back in fright.

"Fogstar, what are you doing? We're supposed to be fi-" Halo started, but Fogstar sent her a glare that made her stop immediately.

"I'm hurting him." Fogstar snapped. Turning his head back to Nightshade. "*We're* hurting him." He gestured to Rebecca, "For what he did… to her." Rebecca didn't know if she agreed with Fogstar's idea of what to do with Nightshade, but Halo's face was even worse. It wasn't quite betrayal, no it was something else, Fogstar shot a cloud at Nightshade who tried to move and block it, but some of it got through anyway. Small lines of black blood trickled down his matted fur. He spat it off and laughed a sick, undefined, blurry laugh that hurt everyone's ears. Fogstar didn't even flinch; she could tell it hurt him, though. She could see how much he wanted revenge now. Nightshade stopped laughing abruptly and turned to Halo.

"Is this how you wanted to get rid of me? Do you really hate me that much?" Halo shook her head and looked to the ground. Her eyes were filled with tears now. Nightshade looked at her pitifully for a second but then looked back over at Fogstar. "So what did I do… to make you this mad?" Fogstar flashed him a look that would've scared anyone; she saw Nightshade flinch under it but he played it off well.

"Stop this army," Fogstar said; he looked out of the corner of his eye at Halo. "Stop it and leave and never come back." But his words were pitifully dull; he knew that it wouldn't stop him. Rebecca didn't know what she was supposed to do. There was no way to get rid of him, she thought. Killing him would make Halo mad and wouldn't be the right choice anyway. Banishing him would kill her, as it did to Abbigail, and rehabilitating him wouldn't be possible at this point. Yet maybe if she wished hard enough it'd work.

"STOP!" She shouted over everyone. Nightshade looked like he wanted to speak but looked at her curiously. "Nightshade... Why?" He looked at her.

"What?"

"Why are you doing this?" Nightshade looked at her; he got the question but kept looking around. Kind of like he didn't understand the answer,

"Cause it's fun?" He asked himself but shook his head. "No, no, not that, hmm. Because I hate her?" He pointed at Halo. "No, no, I don't... yes you do... I... I do?"

"Why would *you* want to do this?"

"You? Or...him? Either? No... you mean... him... he... I-"

"Don't know?" She finished for him. He nodded but kept opening his mouth over and over again, trying to answer the question. Halo smiled sadly from the front of the crowd.

"But... No- no I don't want to... you do but I don't-" He kept shaking his head; she swore his eyes turned crystal again.

"This isn't you," She said as he frowned at her. "You're not yourself. You know that, you keep talking like there are two of you. Please...come back. They miss you, the whole Astral Plane does." He didn't look convinced, so she added. "She misses you." He looked over at Halo, and she sniffled and nodded. The orange in his eyes faded, and he fell out of the sky, hitting the ground with a 'thump.' He held his head in his paws and shook off the painful confusion. Rebecca turned around to look at Fogstar, who was sitting down, looking defeated as if he had failed. She walked up to him as Halo ran over to help Nightshade up.

"You okay?" Rebecca asked, Fogstar flinched and nodded sadly. "Look, thanks for saving me and uh... I respect your choice. You know... not killing him and stuff." He gave a slight smile.

"Sorry," Fogstar said, looking up at Rebecca, she shrugged.

"I understand." She put a hand on his shoulder, and he snuggled into her arms. Everything seemed right with the worlds. Of course, it wasn't, but nobody cared right now.

Tears

Halo spent most of the time explaining what happened to Nightshade through her tears of joy. She kissed him over and over again until he had to push her off, blushing. After a while, beings started to notice that the Nightshade followers weren't going away; they just stood there looking at Nightshade like he had betrayed all of them. At one point a beautiful woman in a lacey black dress and black heels came over to him in a very seductive voice,

"So… what happened to 'I will never turn back to being weak again'? Or 'I will never love anyone'?" She then tried to stab him, which made Halo fling her across Despair. Nightshade followers drowned out her screaming with their goop as they attacked her in the distance. Nightshade eventually got up and looked around in suppressed horror.

"I… I did this?" Halo nodded her head sadly; he looked at her and then at the crowd and then at Rebecca. "W-Who… uh… who is this?"

"I'm Rebecca," Fogstar had his ears pulled back and placed a paw in front of her.

"That's an odd name, isn't it…?" Nightshade said Halo giggled in joyous tears behind him.

"She's the Savior," Fogstar said, looking at him warily. After that, Halo had to explain what they were doing here, as well as 'what those black things are.' He went up to one of his followers and looked at them, poking it with his claw and giving it a disgusted look. It was very offended at this. Halo told him what it was, what it did, and how it came to be. Nightshade had a different expression after that. Once Halo picked up on the fact that the followers were not disappearing, she called a meeting for the council in fifteen minutes.

"They're very different from when you were here last." Halo had added after talking to the man in the suit who was called Communicate.

"How... long has it been?" Nightshade had asked as Halo's face dropped.

"Oh... well, um..." She had brushed Communicate off and stepped towards Nightshade with her head down. "About... a hundred and fifty years..." Nightshade had widened his eyes and nodded quietly. About fifteen minutes later, Halo had called Rebecca and Fogstar and walked them up to the tower toward the courtroom.

"Are you ready?" Halo asked Nightshade outside the door, he nodded his head and took a deep breath. She opened the door slowly to the sound of screams.

Meeting

The girl in the heart dress was screaming in the nurse's lap. The man with the black hole in his head cowered behind the short wall that ran across the room. Clockwork was screaming bloody murder and running around the room with papers flying behind him from the stack in his arms. The golden butterfly was flying close to the top of the room and breathing heavily. When Nightshade tried to speak, they all screamed louder, and most of them got up and ran to the back of the room. Halo rolled her eyes and stepped in front of Nightshade, who looked back at Fogstar with an eyebrow raised. Fogstar growled at him, Nightshade pulled his ears back and looked back down at the floor. Rebecca nudged Fogstar, he looked at her with a face that said, 'what?'

"Okay, stop overreacting," Halo said as the rest of the council calmed down a little. The woman in the nurse outfit spoke up.

"W-Why is *he* here?" She asked, pointing a shaking finger at Nightshade.

"Because he is better now Health, he is... uncorrupted." Halo pulled Nightshade up to stand next to her. He smiled shyly at her and then walked up to the council, who were pushing themselves into the wall.

"Hi... again?" The council screamed, and Clockwork ran out of the room. Fogstar rolled his eyes again and sat down on the wall pulling out what looked like a scroll and starting to write on it.

"HOW IS HE SO CALM?" The man with the white suit screamed at Fogstar, he turned to look at him aggressively.

"If anything I should be the maddest at him, I should want to hurt him... kill him." The council looked at Fogstar with confused and scared eyes; Clockwork poked his head around the corner of the door with the same expression. "I *do* want to kill him." He said, looking up at Nightshade, whose expression was of guilt and terror. "But I haven't. Because I am loyal to Halo, and he..." Fogstar sighed. "got better." Halo nodded thankfully as the rest of the council looked at him they were calmer about Nightshade but must've switched their fear on Fogstar.

"Thank you Fogstar, this is correct, Nightshade, the real Nightshade, is back now. The Nightshade that had followers, the Nightshade that turned so many of us, this isn't him." She pointed at Nightshade. "This is the Nightshade that ruled the Astral Plane alongside me. This is the Nightshade that I love." The council stopped screaming after that. Halo had kept Nightshade's corruption from her council, which raised a million questions about what happened and why he was good all of a sudden. She explained the whole thing, even some parts Rebecca didn't know, and some, surprisingly, Fogstar didn't. Nightshade spoke up in the middle to correct her and give the story in the first person. After that, the council slowly returned to their seats and sat in silence as Fogstar marked some more things down on a scroll.

"Fogstar, that will be enough," Halo said, he stopped writing and set his quill down. He bowed, and the paper folded itself in half and flew across the room to land in a file cabinet. "So… Nightshade about those followers…" But she trailed off when she looked behind her. Nightshade was standing there, with his head down, laughing. Not as much as a laugh, more of a steady chuckle.

"Yes, about those 'Nightshade followers' I am so glad that name stuck, it really is quite… self-explanatory." He said, looking up at Halo now; his eyes were back to that horrible orange color.

"Nightshade?" Halo said, stepping in front of the council members, who were now cowering in the corner. Rebecca transformed and pulled her sword out as Fogstar leaped up and started growling. "Wh-" But Nightshade cut her off.

"You haven't gotten rid of me ya-know? I'm still here and waiting. You'll never get rid of me, and, thanks for flinging

Seducia, I kinda hated her. Ha-ha." He laughed again, this time choking on something. "Those Nightshade followers aren't leaving until I leave, and as I just said, I don't plan on leaving anytime soon." He smiled and put his arms out like you would for a hug. "Have fun with them; trust me, it's not going to end well." His teasing voice slipped as Nightshade turned back into good Nightshade and collapsed back onto the floor. Halo ran over to him and helped him up.

"Are you okay?" She asked he nodded but sniffed up what looked like blood from his nose. Fogstar sat back down, and Rebecca's sword, along with her costume, disappeared.

"w-we have to... uh... well, do something. I don't think this is right... it isn't right, is it?" He asked himself; over and over again until he sat down to quietly decide what he thought was the best thing to do. Halo kept checking on him but refused to let the court leave until he had made a decision, which made everyone else contemplate a decision. He finally snapped his head up, he was breathing fast but quietly with feeble tears in his eyes.

"*I* have to go..." He said, holding a paw up to his chest. "I have to leave."

Plans

"WHAT?" Halo screamed as Nightshade shared his plan.

"I need to lock myself up and take the Nightshade followers with me until you find a way to completely uncorrupt me." He said matter-of-factly staring Halo straight in the eyes.

"B-but." Halo started but stopped short because of the look Nightshade gave her.

"I *have* to." He said, walking up to Halo; a faint smile crossed his face as Halo realized that he was serious and was planning to leave, then she started crying.

"No…" She hugged him and sobbed into his shoulder. Fogstar immediately looked like he regretted all the hate he had for Nightshade. Halo sniffled, but Nightshade reassured her.

"How long was I chained up in there? A hundred years? That's not so long, is it?" Nightshade said, smiling sadly. Halo sniffled and nodded into his furry shoulder.

"No… no, it's not." Halo pulled away from him and wiped tears and traces of black goop off her face.

"Exactly, see." He patted her on the head and smiled. "I'll be back sooner or later, uh… one question." He looked around the council room. "How exactly did you lock me up last time?" Fogstar's ears dropped, the council room had a much less happy atmosphere. "Uh… Something I did, isn't it?" The council room nodded sadly.

"We didn't," Halo said, looking over at Fogstar warily, "Abb-
Our last Savior gave up her life to do so... Instead of
beating you..." Nightshade dropped his ears and cleared his
throat.

"oh..." He said awkwardly, looking around at Fogstar, who
had another expression of suppressed rage. "Well... then
we find a different way."

"Sorry, My Lord, but... how?" The black hole headed man
asked, causing the rest of the room to nod and look
around.

"um... well..." He stopped to think for a second and then
took a deep breath looking up at the rest of the room.
"How long do you need?"

Home?

After the meeting, the council filed out of the room to give
Halo and Nightshade some time to catch up. Fogstar was
pretty mad, and most of the council stayed far away from
him. Rebecca walked with him back through the marble
halls, eventually getting to their room where Fogstar laid
down on the bed in a heap and sighed pitifully.

"Sorry about that..." He said, rolling over on his side.

"It's okay, I understand. I don't think Nightshade did,
though..." Fogstar shot her a look and then turned away in
shame. Rebecca sat down next to him, he glanced up at
her.

"I just… don't know what to do about him. She gave up her *life* because of him and now he's staring me straight in the eye and doing nothing wrong. But he… killed her." Rebecca questioned his thinking, he never killed her. It wasn't his fault for any of this.

"He didn't kill her, not that Nightshade at least," Rebecca said as Fogstar looked up at her.

"I don't really care," he growled. "There needs to be someone to blame, and it was always him."

"Well, blame the other him then. The one that we're locking away, and by the time we get him out again and fix him you better be over her. Besides, he's still going away so you don't have to take out all of your selfish rage on him anymore. And then-" Fogstar cut her off.

"Then, you have to leave…" He trailed off, looking away from her sadly.

"…what?"

"You know, you can't just stay in the Astral Plane, once this is all over you… you have to go home." Rebecca hadn't ever even considered that. She never thought she'd have to leave. The prospect of it scared her now.

"Oh… uh… I have to…" She paused for a second, realizing something, "Will I ever see you again?" Fogstar stared at the ground for a while.

"I don't know…" He said, still staring down. They sat in silence for a while until Halo came into the room.

"Come on… There are things to do…"

Curtains

After following Halo through the halls for a few minutes in silence, she finally looked over her shoulder at them.

"Okay, Fogstar, I know you hate Nightshade, but you don't have to be this quiet. I mean, it's kind of…" Fogstar looked up at her, and she stopped. She had a confused expression and stopped walking. "That's not it, is it?" Fogstar shook his head softly, she sighed, and they kept walking. They rounded a corner and pushed open a pair of doors into a room that Rebecca had never seen before. Fogstar walked off and sat down in the corner. Nightshade sat in the center on a pedestal of white concrete, and the council was dotted around the room watching and waiting. Nightshade looked kind of scared, but seeing Halo, he swallowed it down and held his head up.

"I'm ready." He said, taking a deep breath, Halo nodded and pulled a lever on the wall. The room instantly lit up with light, and Rebecca looked around to see where it was coming from, and it turned out it was just the ceiling lights. Halo walked to where Nightshade was standing and held his paw.

"Are you sure?" She asked, he nodded his head and turned to look at Rebecca.

"Thank you… for waking me up… and Foggy…" Fogstar glared at him from the corner of the room. "I'm sorry." Fogstar looked down at the ground as Halo started the process of locking up Nightshade. It took a very long time, and Halo seemed to be draining energy from everyone to use for Nightshade. When Halo finished, she got up and smiled sadly at Nightshade. Her eyes turned bright white and reflected off the lamps making the room so brilliant Rebecca had to cover her eyes. When she finally opened them, Nightshade was gone, and Halo was looking even sadder than she had before.

The whole council was staring at the ground. Fogstar was the first to get up and pulled Rebecca out of the room, followed by everyone but Halo. They went back up to their room in complete silence. Fogstar sat down in the corner and sulked. Rebecca looked out the white void window, it was strangely calming. A wind she couldn't see blew her hair back quietly. It was the first time in a few days that Rebecca felt like she was actually alone, no Halo, no Fogstar, just her in a room looking out a window. Then she remembered Fogstar was, in fact, there.

"We should get to bed…" He grumbled, stalking over to the bed and laying on the pillow. He pointed at a light switch behind the door. Rebecca walked over to it and switched it off, covering the whole room in darkness as she climbed into bed. The sheets pulled over her outfit, which got surprisingly less filthy every time she transformed. In truth, she felt terrible too; Nightshade had been here for only a few hours, a few hours of being free. Then he had to go back to the depths of his corruption with no way out. He was brave, and even though she thought she'd never say it, he was a good person. She looked up to see Fogstar who must've been thinking the same thing.

"I think you need to forgive him." Fogstar's expression turned to guilt once again and then to anger for which he then looked sorry. "He didn't kill her," She reminded him. He gave her a betrayed look and curled up tighter. They sat like that for a while until sleep carried Rebecca into dreams of floating light and shadows cast on the sorry grounds below.

The white void cast glowing beams across the floor of the room, silent rays of wind blowing the curtains forward. It was a peaceful morning, Rebecca got up noticing her hair was already brushed, and her clothes were clean. She looked around for a bit, trying to find who did it but instead saw that Fogstar was gone. She walked to the door turning the knob and stepping out into the marble hallways for the last time. She finally reached a guard who pointed her in the direction of the kitchens. The large double doors were still there, and when she walked inside, she found the whole council except for Halo and Fogstar sitting inside. They turned their heads to look at her with sorrowful smiles. She sat down, and a waiter came out of the doorway with a feast of astral foods. The council members picked up what they knew they liked and allowed the hands of other members to interweave with theirs, seeking out the correct object and bringing it back to their plates. The man in the white suit with brown hair looked around the table before adding, "We should introduce ourselves? I'm Family," He gave a little bow and looked to his left at the girl in the heart dress.

"Love..." She said, smiling up at her; the girl in the nurse's outfit was Health. The black hole headed man was Mindscape; Strand introduced herself even though she already knew her name. Clockwork skipped his turn and looked to where Fogstar would usually be seated. "I recommend those berries, at least for breakfast..." Love said as Health shot her a look, "Or Tabil Stock, if you want to be healthy." She smiled awkwardly at Health.

"Thanks…" She picked up both and tried them, they were both alright. "Can I get some more of this stuff? It's delicious…" She asked as Mindscape nodded, sending a purple dot that called a waiter over to the table. The door opened, and Fogstar walked through it and sat down. He looked even more of a mess than last night, and it seemed to scare the council members. His fur was matted and dense, and he looked like he had been crying all night.

Heart Head

"What?" Fogstar asked, looking around; his voice was hoarse and shallow. The council members picked up on this, and Health gave him a funny look. He dragged what looked like a plate of salad in front of him and began to eat. The food Rebecca ordered was sat down in front of her as Fogstar looked up before continuing to eat. After Fogstar had sat down, the room took on a much less friendly tone. In fact, it seemed almost depressing. After most of the council members had finished eating, they got up and left, but a few of them, Love, Health, and Strand, stayed behind to talk to Fogstar.

"Are you feeling alright?" Love asked, reaching a hand over to him, Fogstar shot her a look, and Love retreated back to her own seat.

"Health usually asks me that question…" He said, staring at his food.

"You seem sad…" Strand said in her dreamy voice. "Maybe because of what's to come… would you like me to show you?" Health sighed and looked like she would face palm, Love stared down at her plate like she was in the middle of a heated argument.

"Don't you understand that would make it worse?" Fogstar glared at Strand from his seat, and Love gave an uncomfortable glance at Health; it seemed like pleading. Strand, on the other hand, seemed entirely unaware of what she had said and was more than a little taken aback by Fogstar's hostility. "I don't want to know what happens in the future, this is already bad enough. I don't want you to make it worse." He stopped talking at Rebecca's glare, "sorry…" She gave him a pitiful look for what seemed like the millionth time.

"I think we need to talk." She said, Fogstar nodded and followed her out into the hallway. "Fogstar, Nightshade was one thing, I understood that. He caused Abbigail to… well, sacrifice herself." He flinched at the sound of her name, "But the council members? They are the ones who helped you and Halo, when has she ever hurt you or anyone that you-" He cut her off.

"I just don't like them rummaging through my head is all, it's not something serious. I don't hate them I just…" he sighed she could tell he was holding back. He didn't want to be alone again. Rebecca was the only one he ever told, who cared or at least cared enough to listen to him vent about everything.

"Hey… why don't you visit me sometimes?" Fogstar perked up at this idea, "Like in the Physical Realm you could…" She stopped, seeing Halo walking down the hallway with a face that told her it was time to go.

Leaving

It didn't take long to pack since she didn't bring anything with her to the Astral Plane. All she had to do was make a mess of herself, so when she got back it looked like she'd been gone a while. Fogstar watched her from outside the doorway for a while before walking away; she couldn't see his expression. After knotting her hair up and fraying the edges of her shirt, she stepped outside into the lovely feeling of Hope that drowned out her anger over leaving. She didn't know if she would see any of them again, if she would ever be as important as she was right now to anyone else. But as she rounded the corner, right into Halo, the thought left her mind.

"I think you should get a chance to say goodbye to everyone." Halo's sweet voice carried into Rebecca's ears. Fogstar was standing beside her, looking better than he had in days. Halo led them up a few flights of stairs and into a crystal-lined hallway that had guards posted at every interval. Halo took out a set of keys, unlocked a door at the end of the hall. Inside was a room made out of sky. White clouds floated over the morning mist as the blue sky turned brighter with the rising sun. A glowing orb, like a crystal ball, sat in the center of the room. "You'll be taking the train back, it's a bit formal, but you know… The teleports are sickening the first time." Halo said as she walked up to the ball. "Now, where do you live?"

"Uh, there's this forest in Minnesota that we go to for summer," Rebecca said, Fogstar stayed behind smiling at them. "That's where Fogstar... kidnapped me?" Halo gave a curious look at Fogstar, and he laughed, he *laughed*.

"Well then, your friends are waiting at the station, have a good time at home Rebecca. When Nightshade brakes out... we will need you again." This thought swelled her with not only relief but pride. She would be coming back at the very least, and then she would be just as significant. Fogstar led her down to the station quietly, his sudden change in attitude not going unnoticed.

"What's with you being so happy all of a sudden?" Rebecca asked. Fogstar smiled up at her.

"I thought through what you said and...uh well... you heard Halo anyways; you're going to come back and..." She smiled at him; at least he was happy and would be getting to see her again. "I'll still miss you..." He said, his smile fading.

"As you said, I'll be back." Rebecca tried to reassure him, but it didn't seem to make him feel a lot better. He was pathetic, the fact he depended on her so much said a lot about him. She wondered if Abbigail thought the same kind of things as her, she had too. With someone so codependent she had to have gotten fed up at some point.

"Yeah, but how long will it take?" She gave a forced smile for him as they walked down more flights of stairs, which were now tinted pink and white as they reflected clouds that didn't exist. They turned another corner into open space that looked just like a train station, or at least what she thought a train station would look like. The sky was white as pink clouds floated across the holographic filter that made everything sparkle. The train had the same feel; while it wasn't hot pink, it seemed soft and airy. Ara, Blaze, Mistral, and surprisingly Smokescreen, were all talking to each other, Mistral seemed especially happy to see Smokescreen.

"Hey!" Ara's sweet voice rang out as she ran over to give a wet hug to Rebecca; her footsteps were puddles of water.

"Oh boy, you did a good job making yourself look like a mess," Mistral added walking up to her,

"Mistral!" Fogstar said in an annoyed voice from behind her. Blaze made his way towards her as well, causing Ara's puddles to evaporate into the smoky air.

"I heard everything that happened. I'm really sorry I wasn't in town," Blaze said, hanging his head guiltily. "I wish you would've stopped by, but I guess it was good you didn't. A ride was probably more entertaining anyways." Ara smiled and nuzzled his arm, he gave her a grin.

"So… you made it…" Smokescreen said, standing behind the crowd of beings talking to her. He looked better than when she last saw him, at least he wasn't dead like she thought. He smiled at her before backing off with the rest of her friends to let her on the train, which just let out a puff of pink smoke. As she got up and started to walk to the door, Fogstar stopped her. He had more tears in his eyes, but he was still smiling.

"Bye." He said, hugging her tighter than she had ever been hugged before and as the conductor whistled 'All aboard,' he let her go. He didn't move though, he just sat and watched her leave with a blank expression. She stepped through the doorway and sat down in a window seat that was fluffy and pink striped. The glass was tinted white and foggy. It reminded her of Fogstar as the train sped up, and everything outside turned to haze.

She had left the Astral Plane...

Epilogue

Drops of rain spattered the window of the police car, which took her home. It reminded her of Ara, and she knew she was following her home. She just wished Fogstar was there, just a cloud of fog to tell her that he was still here, but it never came. The officer driving her home was a fit man; he was well-mannered and kind enough to listen to her made-up story about where she had been. Rebecca had read enough books to know telling the police you'd been to another dimension was a bad idea. The falling drops of rain outside blurred the view—that and the fact that the car was driving very fast. Rebecca didn't want to go home, she wanted to stay with Fogstar and everyone else in the Astral Plane, she wanted to stay in Hope and help Halo until Nightshade got back. She would, of course, be going back, but now that she thought about it, Fogstar was right. How long would it take for Nightshade to break out again? Last time it was 100 years, how long would it be this time? The officer seemed to notice her distress.

"You okay?" He asked, keeping his eyes on the mirror pointed at her. She nodded slowly and continued staring out the window. He didn't seem convinced. Her diamond necklace bounced with the bumps of the road; it sat waiting for further use. They pulled into the driveway of her house; it was one-story and made of yellow-tinted concrete. Potted plants decorated the ground, and as she got out of the car, she swore they gave little bows to her. Her mother opened the door and rushed out in tears hugging her as hard as anyone ever had; well, except Fogstar, when she had to leave, Rebecca hugged her back. It was a sad thing to see her mother like this; even more, it was tragic that she didn't want to come back. The rain had stopped by now, and the sun had shone its face from behind the clouds. Her brother was sitting in a chair on his phone when she came in; he raised his head to look at her worriedly. She made her way into her room and sat down on her bed as the police talked to her mother. After a while, she came back into the room with a face that said she knew Rebecca was lying.

"Where were you?" Her Mother asked. Rebecca knew she couldn't tell her so instead, she smiled at her and sat up.

"I can't tell you... you wouldn't believe me... when I go back, don't get worried, please, I don't want you to be. I've seen too many people I care about worried about me..." Her mother was confused yet being smart decided that it would make a good conversation for dinner, she nodded and left. The Astral Plane was waiting for her, and it would remain. But she would be back; she would never give up on them.

Authors Note:

Special Thanks to:

My Mother, for pushing me to finish this writing project and helping to do the editing.

My Father, for letting me use his computer to write.

My Brother, for giving truthful criticism and helping me to improve.

My Friends, for being supportive and giving me new people to put in this book, thank you butterfly.

Emma Jai McDonald, for cover art and the plot of the next book.

And to everyone who read this and tested it out to see what was wrong or could be better.

Thank you for reading Personification and I hope you enjoy the next installments.

www.ingramcontent.com/pod-product-compliance
Lightning Source LLC
Chambersburg PA
CBHW020930160726
47993CB00005B/2214